The Kn

Bound together by their oaths and by friendship...

Brave and talented knights Leopold, Hugh and Tristan are determined to serve their king and country. They are destined to be the greatest warriors in all the lands, but their reputations are risked by a jealous enemy. Now they must each complete a task lest they lose their knighthoods. But as each knight sets off on their individual missions, they find themselves embarking on the greatest of quests—love.

Follow these valiant warriors and the women who have captured their hearts!

Read Leopold and Arianwen's story in

The Knight's Rebellious Maiden

And look out for Hugh's and Tristan's stories

Coming soon!

Author Note

Thank you for picking up Leo and Ari's story.

Leo and Ari were such a fun couple to write about. They are both passionate and equally stubborn; they butt heads but also love chatting to each other.

The events in the novel take place in 1337 and in the same world as my King's Knights series. I loved returning to this time period and thinking of new, exciting missions for my heroes. This time, I've set Leo and Ari's story in Wales. It begins in my hometown, Abertawe (Swansea in English), and moves across the beautiful Welsh countryside to a fictional castle in Pembrokeshire. It was great using places I've visited for inspiration in this story and meant I could drag my family out for walks and call it research. I hope you enjoy reading the novel as much as I enjoyed writing it.

If you'd like to sign up to my newsletter for freebies, bonus chapters and deleted scenes, then please visit my website, www.ellamatthews.co.uk.

The Knight's Rebellious Maiden

———

ELLA MATTHEWS

HARLEQUIN
HISTORICAL

Recycling programs
for this product may
not exist in your area.

ISBN-13: 978-1-335-59617-8

The Knight's Rebellious Maiden

Copyright © 2024 by Ella Matthews

Harlequin Enterprises ULC
22 Adelaide St. West, 41st Floor
Toronto, Ontario M5H 4E3, Canada
www.Harlequin.com

Printed in U.S.A.

Ella Matthews lives and works in beautiful South Wales. When not thinking about handsome heroes, she can be found walking along the coast with her husband and their two children (probably still thinking about heroes, but at least pretending to be interested in everyone else).

Chapter One

Wales, July 1337

Sir Leopold dropped the three ales onto the table with a satisfying clunk.

'Watch it, Leo,' muttered Hugh as some of the drink spilled onto his lap. Leo would normally apologise for his uncharacteristic clumsiness, but he couldn't muster his usual enthusiasm to speak. This wasn't their last drink before facing the gallows, but it felt like it.

The three men picked up their tankards. Like most of their movements, it was done in unison; they worked well together even in this. Without these two men, the past fourteen years would have been hell for Leo. Together, they had formed a bond that was tighter than brotherhood. Leo would die for Hugh and Tristan and he knew the feeling was mutual, although they would perhaps express it in less passionate terms. He was the dramatic one of the three of them, after all.

'This will all be over before we know it. We'll be successful, because we always are, and we'll be back on our chosen path before the summer is out,' said Tristan, rubbing his upper lip as he put his drink down on the rough-hewn surface.

Leo appreciated Tristan's trying to rally their spirits but his friend's optimism wasn't working on him. It was hard to look on the bright side when everything had gone so wrong. Here they were, arguably the best knights produced in decades, stuck in the back end of nowhere, each on individual soul-destroying, pointless missions when they all should have been on their way to Windsor to join the ranks of the elite knights. Leo smoothed his beard. They were here because of petty jealousy, which could easily have been avoided if only the three of them had paid attention to those who wished them ill. It was a lesson learned, but the price had been steep—far higher than any of them had wanted to pay.

'At least we're away from Lord Ormand. He can't touch us here,' said Hugh.

Leo nodded in agreement. That was one of the only positives in this whole mess: being away from the lord who'd trained them into knighthood since they were seven years old—or at least the man who had allowed them to reside at his castle while other people did the job he was supposed to do. Lord Ormand had proved to be as obstinate as he was vindictive, worse even than Leo's parents, who only found him disinteresting rather than a source of constant irritation. Lord Ormand had not taken well to the three of them being so much better than him at everything, which was the main reason they were here and not following the path they had set out for themselves as soon as they'd been old enough to plan.

Leo stared into his tankard. It was already half-empty; he was drinking far quicker than he normally would and he should stop. He would in a moment when the gut-churning sensation of failure had settled. He took another slug and another, but it did nothing to stop the inner voice—which sounded suspiciously like his father—telling him that of course this had happened to him because he was not skilled or clever enough. That if only he was more like his brother—studious, pious and less hot-headed—none of this would have happened. His only hope was that his imaginings did not become reality, that he didn't have to listen to this sermon in real life. Bad news travelled fast and so it was an unrealistic hope that his parents wouldn't find out, but hopefully he could sort the situation out so that he could visit them with his head held high. Otherwise, it would only confirm their belief that he was the lesser son, the second born who would never amount to anything much. He had spent his whole life trying to prove otherwise, and he'd been so close. But now this.

'I don't know why you look so grim, Leo,' said Hugh. 'Your task is not as onerous as ours. All you must do is escort one bride-to-be to her new home. You could do that in your sleep. It will take you a week at most.'

'It's demeaning.'

After all the praise heaped on his fighting ability in the past few years by his instructors—an ability he had honed precisely to avoid ending up in a position such as this—this was what it had led to. Yes, it was true that the whole mission should only take him fewer than ten days—possibly even fewer if he could get the lady to ride quickly—but that didn't mean he wasn't humiliated by the task. And if his family found out it would confirm everything they thought about him and possibly worse.

Still, if his mission did take him that short amount of time, he could travel to help Tristan with his task. They could then rendezvous with Hugh, and the three of them could be in Windsor within a couple of months.

Leo took another swig of ale, trying not to get his hopes up. Lady Arianwen had probably never left the safety of her castle before and may not know the front of a horse from the back. Ten days, then; twenty at most. It was best to hope for Windsor inside of three months. That was all it would take. It was nothing set against the entirety of his life. Lord Ormand may have declared that success in their missions was their only way to progress further as knights, but he wanted them demeaned and delayed, and sending them to Wales had been a good way to do that. But Lord Ormand was not going to succeed in his attempts to destroy their spirits because Leo was not going to fail and neither were his closest friends. He would become the warrior he had promised himself he would be when nobody in his family had seen his worth. Nothing and nobody would stand in his way.

'We can't afford to make any mistakes,' he said, tracing the tankard's handle with his thumb.

'We haven't made any mistakes yet,' Tristan reminded him.

'Indeed, we have not,' countered Hugh, his frown fierce against the injustice of their situation.

Leo shook his head. They *had* made a grave error, and they were paying for it.

'We underestimated Lord Ormand and that petty, ridiculous little twerp, Robert, and how much they both hated us.' He drained the rest of his drink. 'We must never make such a miscalculation again.'

'To be fair,' said Tristan, pushing back his chair and standing, his own empty tankard gripped in his hand, 'I always knew they hated me. I just didn't realise they despised you two to the same extent.'

'If only you didn't have such a pretty face,' said Hugh, his eyes twinkling, amusement replacing his annoyance.

Tristan made a rude hand gesture as Hugh and Leo sniggered. It didn't matter how dire the situation, ribbing Tristan about his looks was always good entertainment. Tristan glared at them, which only caused them to laugh harder.

'It wasn't his fault Lady Cassandra became so smitten with him,' Hugh commented, ever the peacemaker, as Tristan made his way over to the landlord to collect more ale. 'Or her daughter.'

Leo grunted in acknowledgement. He knew Tristan had not been at fault and, even if he had been, Tristan was closer to him than family, and Leo would side with him until death.

'You can't hold it against him. He did everything to avoid them.' Hugh was always the earnest one, the honourable one, the one who wanted to be fair to everyone. It would pain him to think that Leo thought badly of Tristan for something completely out of the man's control.

'I know. I don't blame him for our current situation,' Leo reassured him. That women threw themselves at Tristan was not something the man encouraged, Leo knew, but it hadn't helped the jealousy of the other men who trained with the three of them. It had only got worse as Tristan had grown older and he had come to the attention of those of superior birth—the women of the castle in which they had all trained.

That Leo was a superior fighter and Hugh cleverer than most had made the grudging resentment of their fellow trainees worse. But maybe their situation wouldn't have been quite so bad if it hadn't been for the obvious adoration of the lord's wife and daughter. The way the two women had followed Tristan around had been painfully embarrassing. Tristan had tried to avoid them, and Leo and Hugh had helped him the best they could, shielding him whenever possible, but it had been to no avail. Lord Ormand hadn't taken long to realise what was happening, but perhaps the situation could still have been saved if Robert, one of their fellow squires, hadn't wanted Lord Ormand's daughter for himself. Robert had gone out of his way to make life difficult for Tristan, becoming more vindictive as the women's admiration became ever more obvious.

And then there had been *the* incident—the casual destruction of a gift Lord Ormand had commissioned for the king only a day after Leo, Hugh and Tristan had undergone the final ceremony to officially become knights. It was the destroyed gift that had brought things to a critical point. Lord Ormand had been unable to find any proof that the three of them had had anything to do with it, because they hadn't. As much as they disliked their lord, they took their responsibilities as chivalric knights seriously. To do something like that went against everything in which all three of them believed—a point they had stressed vigorously. But they had still been blamed, the animosity that surrounded them too great for anyone to accept their assertions of innocence.

Leo was convinced that Robert was behind the vandalism, carried out with the intention of blackening

Tristan's name, but he could find nothing to implicate the man or anyone else. Lord Ormand's rage had been both cruel and unfair, targeting not only Tristan, whom he had come to hate beyond measure, but also the two men closest to him whom Lord Ormand had already despised for besting him at every skill in which the three of them had trained since they had turned fourteen.

Only the high status of their family names had saved them from total banishment, which was galling in itself because Leo's family had shown no interest in him for many years. Leo sometimes wondered if they remembered his existence, although he had no doubt they would recall him instantly once they learned of all that had passed.

'At least we have Sir Benedictus's offer to sustain us.'

Leo grunted. Desperate to avoid the ignominy of their punishment, Leo had written to Sir Benedictus, the leader of the King's Knights and one of the most powerful men in the country, asking him to intervene on their behalf. The letter he had received in response had been encouraging despite its brevity. 'It is better than nothing,' Leo agreed.

'It is good, Leo.'

'So long as we all complete our missions successfully.'

'We will.'

Leo rubbed his chin, the bristles of his short beard scraping the pads of his fingers. 'As the most senior knight, you'd have thought he could...'

But Hugh was shaking his head. 'He cannot go against Lord Ormand's decree. Even you must be able to see that undermining the King's Barons is a terrible tactical decision.'

Leo didn't bristle at the *even you* comment. Out of the three of them, he knew he was the most hot-headed, the most likely to rush into action without thinking. His quick reflexes had saved them more times than seemed possible, and his brother knights relied on his instincts just as he depended on them to rein him in when needed.

There was nothing Sir Benedictus could currently do, but he had made them a promise. If the three of them completed their missions for Lord Ormand successfully, Sir Benedictus would receive them at Windsor. He would be willing to assess their abilities and if he was impressed with the three of them, he would request their transfer from Lord Ormand's service to his. It was more than they had dared to hope for but the emphasis on Sir Benedictus's insistence that it be the three of them who needed to present themselves at Windsor made Leo nervous. He could not bear to be the weak link in the group; he could not let his friends down just as he knew they would not let him down, either.

Leo glanced at Tristan, who was walking back to their table with more ales. He appeared to be irresistible to women. Even now, the barmaid was watching Tristan with undisguised longing on her face, although Leo knew Tristan would have done nothing to encourage it except talk to her courteously.

'Here,' said Tristan, thrusting tankards at them. He was frowning, which did nothing to mar his almost perfect features. 'I want you to know I did everything I could to put Lady Cassandra and her daughter off me. I didn't—'

'We know,' said Leo, because he did, and because he could see how anguished Tristan was at the thought that his friends might blame him for their current predicament. Leo would hate Tristan to think, even for a moment, that he blamed him for anything. Tristan believed in Leo, and had supported him whenever Leo's belief in himself had failed.

'As Hugh says, we'll be back to following our plan before we know it.'

Leo knew he was not just trying to reassure Tristan. He wanted—no, he *had*—to believe that they would all succeed over the next few weeks. If they didn't, then he would have to become a common soldier or a sword for hire, and his parents would probably disown him for the shame of his failure. They already had their older son, the heir, the golden boy, the one who was already a knight by virtue of order of birth rather than skill. Leo would go down in history as the only son from the Beauvarlet family ever to fail at the duties of knighthood. He straightened in his seat. No, the plan had to work. It was simple enough: become the best knights in the land, join the illustrious King's Knights as elite warriors and gain the respect of King Edward, the entire court and their own respective families. Leo knew he had the most to prove. He was the only one of the three whose parents thought so little of him. Their plan was simple and had been going straightforwardly...until it wasn't.

Leo drained his tankard. To get this mission over with, it had to begin and he was the nearest to the start of his. It was only a short ride from this tavern to Abertawe Castle, where the Lady Arianwen resided. He stood. 'Tristan, I will see you in St David's in twelve days. If you have not completed your mission, I will assist you and then we will travel together to meet you, Hugh.' Twelve days would have to be enough. Lady Arianwen would learn to ride like the wind whether she liked it or not. 'Hugh, we will come to you when we are both done. Godspeed to you both.'

They raised their tankards towards him as he strode from the tavern. He didn't look back. They had a plan and he wasn't going to be the one who let the others down. He *must* succeed. His pride, his whole future, and that of his friends, was depending on it.

He hoped Lady Arianwen was ready to go because there was no time to waste.

Chapter Two

'They say Sir Leopold is the best fighter ever trained,' said Ari's mother as she pulled Ari's braid tight.

Ari made a sound that she hoped indicated she was interested and attending to her mother's conversation but that she had no further comment to make. It must have been relatively convincing because her mother carried on while Ari stared out the window.

'He is said to have fought ten men at once. Can you imagine such a thing?' Ari could and frequently did, although it was not this faceless knight in her imaginings but herself. A flicker of resentment curled in Ari's stomach at the way her mother revered this unknown knight but did not recognise her own daughter's skill. She tamped down the feeling. Her mama never meant to be cruel and Ari would not sully their last moments together with bitterness. 'Wouldn't it be wonderful to see Sir Leopold in action? I did ask Lord Owain ap Llewellyn if we could hold a tournament so we could see a display of his prowess but he said there wasn't time.'

Ari wasn't surprised. Lord Owain ap Llewellyn, her stepfather, was as desperate for Ari to be gone as she was to leave. So much so, that when the maidservant originally meant to travel with them had come down with the grippe, he had not wanted to delay Ari's journey by waiting for her to recover. Travelling without one suited Ari's plans and so she had not argued. Her dowry, a chest of linens, coins and a small amount of jewellery, had gone on ahead of her, so that they would not draw attention to themselves as they travelled through the countryside. There was nothing to keep her here or slow down her journey. Lord Owain would want her to depart almost as soon as Sir Leopold arrived, and that didn't hurt her because it was exactly what she wanted, too.

Sir Leopold was meant to be arriving any day now to escort her to her new home. The residents of Abertawe Castle were in a flutter about seeing the young knight in the flesh after a recent travelling bard had told them stories of his accomplishments. Her stepfather, in particular, was bursting with pride that his family was being awarded the honour of Sir Leopold's escort, but Ari could not understand why. If Sir Leopold was as spectacular as it was rumoured, then why had he been sent to this backwater to escort her? She wasn't even a real daughter of Lord Owain's, and Abertawe was so very far away from the seat of British power that it made no sense to her. If this knight was as good as the bards suggested, then he should be in Windsor where the real action was. Ari suspected news of his skill had been greatly exaggerated as it had made its way across the country. She certainly hoped so because it suited her plans if he turned out to be incompetent.

'There. You're ready.' Her mother patted her shoulders and let out a gentle sigh. 'Your father will be so proud of you.'

Ari laid a hand over her mother's and turned to smile up at her even as her stomach twisted. Her mother had been calling Lord Owain ap Llewellyn her father for the past couple of years. Ari hated it. Her real father, the estimable David Fletcher, might be long dead but that didn't mean he had not existed—despite her mother's best efforts to erase his memory. She hadn't mentioned his name in years. This insistence on referring to her stepfather as her father hurt Ari more than she could put into words. She had tried so many times to tell her mother that, until she'd realised it was pointless.

Lady Katherine was sweet and placid—the exact opposite of Ari. To argue with her was like kicking a puppy, a vile thing to do. Years ago, Ari had tried to make her voice heard but in speaking what was in her heart, it had seemed that her words only hurt her mother, and Ari hated to see her mother upset. So she kept her comments inside her, kept her feelings locked away, pretending, as always, to be someone she wasn't. To tell the truth before she left would only make her mother cry, and Ari did not want that to be their last moment together.

The truth was that her real father would not be proud of this moment. Her father had been the head man-at-arms of this castle. He had seen Ari's potential, had known that Ari was not meant to follow the traditional route laid out for a woman, that she was too good a swordswoman to waste herself on marriage. He had wanted something different for his daughter. He had wanted her to become one of the very few female warriors. Up until his death in Ari's fourteenth year, her papa had trained her as if she were a page and then a squire of this castle. She had learned to fight with a sword and bow and to ride like she was born to the saddle. She had bested the boys who trained alongside her and then started besting the young knights her father pitted her against. Fighting made her blood sing, and she had wanted nothing more than to spend her life on the battlefield where she could use her skills and become the best, like her father had done before he had become head man-at-arms. Everything changed before her fifteenth summer when her beloved papa had died. Bewildered, Ari had not been able to understand why her mother had remarried only months afterwards, this time to the lord of the castle, a man who had been so taken with Lady Katherine's beauty that he had married beneath him in order to have her for himself.

'I am so glad you and your father are on better terms now, Ari,' her mother said, gently sweeping her hand down Ari's braid. 'I am so proud of the woman you have become.'

An unwelcome lump formed in Ari's throat and she swallowed, trying to dislodge it. If her mama knew what Ari was planning to do once she left Abertawe Castle, she would be horrified. Ari was going to betray the only person who loved her, but if she didn't then she would live a life of misery. Even now, she wanted to correct her mother, to remind her that Lord Owain was her stepfather only, but she held her tongue.

'I know you thought your life would be spent on the battlefield, my darling,' her mother continued, 'but I hope you can see that the life your father has chosen for you is the better option. You will have a castle and a family of your own.'

Ari pressed her lips tightly together, to keep the scream building up inside her from escaping. The life Lord Owain had mapped out for her was not the one she wanted, but there was no point in saying that. Her mother had never heeded Ari's protestations, so why would she now? Her stepfather had very firm ideas about what a woman should and shouldn't do: a woman should not ride a horse unless it was to travel somewhere and certainly never in a tournament; she definitely should not wield a sword nor shoot an arrow, or follow any other pursuit outside of the limited domestic sphere of her existence.

Ari had been oppressed for so long, but she had never let go of her dream. She would become a warrior, just as she and her real father had planned.

'Do you ever think of Papa?' asked Ari before she could think better of it.

'Of course I think of David, Ari.' Ari closed her eyes at the mention of her father's first name on her mother's lips. 'He was a special man and he will always have a place in my heart. He would be proud of you, too, even with his unusual ideas for your future.' In the months following her mother's marriage to Lord Owain, Ari had tried to argue the case for her to remain training with the squires, but it had been in vain. Lord Owain did not want it, and her mother either didn't or couldn't counter her new husband's decree. Regardless, Ari had carried on practising her moves, though only in private or secluded spaces; her sparring was therefore rusty, but she had done the best she could under the circumstances.

Ari couldn't even resent her mother for not sticking up for her; her mama was by her nature sweetly soft and gentle. Instead, all her ire was focused on the man her mother had married.

'Do you have any questions about your marriage, my dear?' asked her mother, moving away from her and re-arranging some pots on the table, her thin fingers flutter-ing slightly, the brief mention of Papa already forgotten.

'No, Mama.' As the daughter of the castle's head man-at-arms, her status had been elevated beyond the com-mon servants but not enough for their family to have their own suite of rooms. Sleeping in the Great Hall with the others had given her a reasonable idea of what went on between a man and a woman—grunting and moan-ing and moving together, as far as she could work out. She did not need to know any further details because her marriage would not take place.

Her mother turned back to her, brushing her hand against Ari's cheek. 'I am sad that Lord Cradoc is so much older than you, but the proximity of his lands means you will be close enough to us so that I can see you again. I'm sure he will behave more amicably to-wards you than he did during that brief visit earlier this year. Once you are married and get to know one an-other better, all will be well.' A slight frown creased her mother's forehead, the only sign that she wasn't entirely sure her words were the truth.

'I am sure Lord Cradoc will be all that is gracious and noble.' Ari said the words her mother wanted to hear but she did not believe them. Ari had met the man once at a feast that had been held to celebrate their be-trothal and they had both attended. Lord Cradoc's icy gaze had travelled over her body, leaving her chilled to the bone. He'd turned away from her without comment and, in that moment, Ari had known that, even without her escape plan, she would not marry a man who could not even deign to speak to the woman he was intending to marry. It didn't matter if he would make the best or the worst of husbands because Ari had no intention of wedding herself to a sour man old enough to be her grandsire. If she'd accepted for a moment that the marriage would truly go ahead then she would have protested vigorously.

As it happened, this marriage presented the ideal opportunity for escape, and she had been waiting for just such a thing for a while. Her plan was simple enough: during this journey to Lord Cradoc's lands in Pembroke, she would find an opportunity to escape the knight who escorted her. He may be rumoured to be an excellent knight but if he was that good, wouldn't he be serving the king instead of being sent to this backwater to escort a nobody to her wedding? Besides, Ari had been trained by her father and she knew that, in his prime, he had been the late king's most trusted man-at-arms. He had trained his majesty's most elite warriors in the art of battle, and before he died he had passed on that skill to her, and she would use it when the time came.

She had gathered everything she needed to start the new life that she wanted. She was going to leave Abertawe Castle as Lady Arianwen and when she ditched her escort she would become Sir Rhys, a Welsh knight who would take the world by storm. She had a secret bag packed containing men's clothing. She would eventually need to buy chainmail, and had coins sown into her clothing to help with that. Smiling genuinely now, she stood and took her mother's hands in hers.

'You have been good to me, Mama. I am going to miss you so.' This was the one part of Ari's plan that stung. Despite their wildly different personalities, Ari loved her mother, and the thought of never seeing her again had caused many sleepless nights. But it could not be helped. Lady Katherine had supported her new husband's wish that Ari marry Lord Cradoc, and Ari would rather die than let that happen.

'Oh, but you are not going so very far away. Pembroke is less than a week's ride. I am sure we will see each other again.' Ari squeezed her mother's hands as her voice broke; she did not like to be far away from her children. It was good that she had several young daughters and another child on the way to take her mind off Ari's absence. Hopefully, when she discovered that Ari was much farther away than Pembroke, that she had not gone through with her wedding, she would have her hands and mind full of her other children and she would not mourn overmuch the daughter who had caused so much strife with her second husband.

A noise sounded in the courtyard below, drawing both ladies' attention to the window. Far below them, a stranger brought his horse to a stop.

'That must be Sir Leopold,' said her mother breathlessly. 'I will go down and greet him with your father.'

Ari pressed her lips together. It would be such a relief when she no longer had to pretend to be content and happy with this life of near captivity. For days now, it had felt as if her skin were too tight for her body, as if she were about to burst free and fly away. She was so close to freedom she could almost touch it, and yet...

There was so much that could still go wrong. She

could lose her nerve. Her sword skills and lack of progress in her sparring might let her down—was she perhaps not as good a fighter as she thought she was? Or alternatively, Sir Leopold could foil her plan at any moment. She was taking a huge risk from which there would be no turning back because she truly believed the end result would be worth it, but her success required great sacrifice. She would never see her mother again after tomorrow, never know her sisters as they grew up. To them she would be the sister who mysteriously vanished—and was presumed dead—and it hurt that they would never know her, either. But to keep in touch would put Ari at too great a risk of discovery.

If she wanted to be true to herself—and she really did—then she would have to make this emotional sacrifice and live with the consequences. She had spent endless days mulling over her decision, and she knew that the result would be worth the pain.

Her mother's footsteps faded into the distance as Ari watched the knight below.

So this was Sir Leopold.

He was a near-mythical warrior if the travelling bards were to be believed, a man whose real character was a mystery she would have to unravel if she wanted her plan to run smoothly.

The knight *did* have a good seat and he *was* controlling his large stallion with ease but that did not mean he was a superior fighter. He swung his leg over and dropped to the ground. Fine, so he was tall, too, and clearly knew his way around a horse. But that still did not mean that all that was said about him was true. She needed him to be so much less than his reputation. She had to get away from him, and the less competent he was, the easier her life would be. She would still get away from him no matter what his skill level because no other outcome was acceptable. Short of committing murder, she would do anything to achieve her goal.

She assessed him from her vantage point above the courtyard. Broad shoulders tapered down to a thin waist; long legs strode purposefully. His was a body meant for warfare, and she could believe that the tales of his prowess might not have been exaggerated. This was a disaster...worse than her worst imaginings. And yet... And yet it was hard to tear her gaze away from him. None of the men who had trained or worked at Abertawe Castle had half of his physical presence. Ari had never seen anyone like him.

His sandy-coloured hair escaped from its loose binding, the wind catching the shoulder-length strands as he pushed it away from his face. As he did so, he looked up and his gaze met hers. For a long moment, they stared at each other. Her heart contracted painfully—once, twice, a third time. The power in his gaze held her still. Her mind screamed at her to move but she was like a fly caught in a web, unable to wrench herself away.

His horse nudged his back, breaking his attention, and he turned slightly, ending whatever spell he'd had over her. Before he could turn back, she pulled herself away from the window, striding quickly to the centre of her chamber, her heart hammering. She pressed her hand to her chest.

Why on earth was it going so fast? Was it because of who he was?

It had to be, for there was no other reason her body

would react in such a way. Whatever the reason was, she did not like it. She would have to ensure it never happened again.

Chapter Three

Leo turned back to his horse, Bosco, and fumbled with the bridle. For the first time in his life, his fingers were not quite following his commands. He slowed, letting out a long breath as his hands steadied. *That* had never happened to him before. Never had he lost control of his actions after a shared glance with a woman. He'd barely even noticed women before now.

He closed his eyes tightly.

Please let that vision in the window not be Lady Arianwen.

He could not react like that to a woman who was going to be under his protection. He was a warrior, and warriors did not stumble after a glance from a woman. It was as if, as soon as he'd caught sight of her, an invisible rope had held him in place, refusing to let him move, and that was ridiculous. Romantic entanglements—hell, any sort of entanglements—were a distraction he did not need. Thank goodness Bosco had nudged him, snapping him out of his reverie before anyone had seen him acting like such a fool over a woman he could barely make out through the warped glass of her window.

He held himself still for a few more beats but the pull

was too great. He needed to know if the woman was still watching him. Before he could talk himself out of it, he lifted his head, but she'd gone. That was a good thing. There was no need for the strange punch to his gut. He was being beyond foolish, almost as bad as the trail of women that fawned over Tristan.

He scrubbed a hand over his face. His strange reaction was probably due to the two ales he'd had earlier. Although they hadn't seemed strong at the time, it was a far better explanation for his faltering with the reins than that he had been mesmerised by a woman.

He'd seen men lose their minds over women, had seen women act without any of their normal sense when they caught sight of Tristan, but he'd never once been troubled by such desires. He'd had only one liaison, which had happened more because he'd felt he should engage in a flirtation with a woman since that was something other men did, rather than as a result of feeling anything special for the woman. It had been disastrous. He tried never to think about it because whenever he did, his stomach twisted into painful knots, his humiliation burning him from the inside. He hadn't realised the woman was using him merely for her own ends until it was too late, and if he could expunge the whole experience from his mind, he would. Since then, he'd not engaged with women much; his life had been spent mostly in training. Perhaps it was not something he should have been so cavalier about after all. If he'd had more experience with women then he'd know whether this reaction was because he was drunk or…something else.

If the woman in the window was indeed Lady Arianwen, if one look robbed him of his senses, then how would he fare over the course of a ten-day journey? Would he be dropping his reins every time she spoke to him? He squared his shoulders. No, of course he wouldn't. He was disciplined and focused, and completing this mission successfully meant everything to him. It didn't matter if the woman in the window was Lady Arianwen. He was in charge of his emotions, and if he decided he would not desire her then he wouldn't. He had been working towards becoming one of the most respected knights in the land since he'd been old enough to understand what that meant, and one beautiful woman was not going to destroy that plan. It wasn't like he was a young lad who'd never spoken to a woman before; he was inexperienced with relationships with the opposite sex but not with discipline and self-control. He was a master at setting his mind to his task and completing it successfully. Whoever his companion was, he would have no difficulty in carrying out his mission. He *could not* have any difficulty in carrying out his mission. Any other outcome was inconceivable.

He tugged Bosco's reins. He would see his horse settled and then make himself known to the lord. Hopefully, he and Lady Arianwen could start their journey tomorrow. The sooner this had begun, the sooner it would be over.

'Aye,' muttered a stout man who had come to stand next to him. 'It gets to all young men at some point. Sometimes the old 'uns, too.'

Leo frowned. Who was this man and what was he talking about? Leo glanced around; he was the only one standing there and so the stranger must be addressing him. 'What does?'

'Lady Arianwen's beauty. You're not the first man to be dazed by such a face.'

Heat spread over Leo's skin. He'd not thought anyone had been watching him. And, hell, that vision at the window *was* Lady Arianwen. He rubbed his forehead. This was going to be a difficult few days. He could not afford to act like a fool every time he glanced at her. They would get nowhere if he acted like a mesmerised boy every time he looked in her direction. 'I'm not daze—'

But the man wasn't listening. 'Born to the late man-at-arms was Lady Arianwen. Sad it was when he died. He was a good man—had some strange ideas but a good man nonetheless.' He continued, 'The mother's the same. Quite breathtakingly beautiful and the lord had to have her for himself. Many a man's lost his mind over the two of them. Shame the young lady's going to be some old man's wife, but if she's lucky he'll die soon and she'll have the pick of whoever she wants after that.'

Leo rubbed Bosco's neck, unsure of how to respond. It was not Leo's business what happened to Lady Arianwen now or in the future. He could not afford to care. All Leo had to do was get her safely from one place to another, so he only nodded. 'The stables are that way,' the man finished. 'I assume that's what you're after.'

'Aye. I appreciate your help.'

But the man was already walking away from him, muttering about foolish strangers who should know better than to become disoriented by a young lass. Leo groaned softly. It was bad enough news that the woman in the window was Lady Arianwen, but worse that someone had noticed his reaction to her. The only positive was that his friends were not with him. It would have been beyond humiliating if Hugh and Tristan had witnessed that. They would tease him about it mercilessly for the rest of his life.

Before he could reach the stable, a richly dressed couple emerged from an ornate doorway, beaming at him as if they were great friends instead of complete strangers.

'Welcome, welcome! You must be Sir Leopold. I am Owain ap Llewellyn, Lord of Abertawe Castle, and this is my lovely wife.'

Lord Owain was a robust man, Leo noted, as he gestured to the woman next to him. She had the same dark hair as the woman in the window, although it was greying around the temples. She would have been astoundingly beautiful in her younger years and even now had the sort of faded beauty about which men would compose poems. 'We are so pleased to welcome you here. The tales of your prowess have reached us, even as far away as we are. We are honoured that you are to escort our beloved daughter to her new home.'

'Yes, yes, so honoured,' echoed Lady Katherine, her smile a mirror of her husband's. Lord Owain carried on, words tumbling out of him so quickly that Leo couldn't keep up. Beside him, his wife nodded along, agreeing with everything her husband said.

Leo sensed movement behind them and everything inside his body sparked. He didn't need to lift his gaze to know that Lady Arianwen had joined them. Hell, if this was how he reacted to her mere presence, their time together was going to be incredibly uncomfortable.

'This is our daughter, Lady Arianwen,' said Lord Owain, gesturing behind him, his smile dipping ever so slightly before returning to full beam.

Leo turned slowly, hoping she wasn't as lovely up close, hoping that somehow the window had distorted her looks and that the old man had been talking nonsense. He grimaced as his gaze settled on her. In the flesh, Lady Arianwen was taller than he'd guessed, only a head shorter than himself. Long, dark hair was braided around the crown of her head, while the rest of it fell around her shoulders. Rich, dark eyes stared frankly back at him, as if she was assessing him and his abilities. She was every bit as stunning as his worst fears had imagined. His heart stilled before racing incomprehensibly fast. A thin tendril of hair curled at the base of her throat and he clenched his fists to stop himself reaching over and brushing it away. He nodded his head towards her. 'Lady Arianwen.'

'Sir Leopold,' she answered softly, her voice sending a shiver down his spine. He held himself still, keeping his lips flat to stop himself from smiling foolishly at her.

Pleased he'd navigated talking to her without giving any indication how attractive he found her, he turned back to her parents and began a discussion about when Lady Arianwen would be ready to leave. That he was aware of her presence during the whole conversation was annoying but he managed not to let his gaze wander, keeping his eyes fixed on the lord and his wife. Next time he saw her, he would be prepared for the shock of her beauty and it would not have such an effect on him; he would make sure of that. Because, stunning woman or not, he was not going to behave like Lady Cassandra and her daughter. He would not be distracted by good looks. He would not suddenly start mooning after someone he could not have. He would not allow himself to do that.

* * *

Ari clasped her hands demurely in front of her in a way she knew pleased her stepfather as they all made their way into the Great Hall. She glanced sideways at the hulking great warrior who was striding along next to her, latent power in every step he took. His gaze darted about the Hall, taking in the long wooden tables, the rich tapestries that Lord Owain preferred and the servants scurrying about. She wondered what he was taking in from the scene. His gaze slid sideways to her then quickly looked away. Heat burned her skin at being caught staring.

As they reached the dais, Ari tried to arrange it so that she was placed next to her mother but, at the last moment, Lord Owain blocked her and she ended up sitting in the chair to the left of him instead. Sir Leopold lowered himself into one to her right, the wood creaking ominously as he settled. Ari doubted anyone so large had ever used it before and she wondered whether it would take his weight. He seemed to be thinking the same thing because he shot her a quick smile, which pinged in her chest like a small arrow.

'I trust you had an uneventful journey to Abertawe,' she commented because she felt some words were needed between them lest they fall into a cavernous pit of strained silence.

'It was,' came his uninspiring reply. Normally, faced with an unenthusiastic response, she would back away from a conversation, but she needed to find out more about this knight from whom she was going to have to escape.

'Have you travelled to Pembroke before?'

'Never.' His voice was deep and gravelly and caused something hot to unfurl in her stomach, something she had never felt before. She began to heap food onto her trencher in the hope that the distraction would make the sensation go away.

Fortunately, Lord Owain heard Sir Leopold's response and spent the next few moments going through the various options on how to travel the relatively short distance to Pembroke. Ari let the words flow over her, helping herself to the various meats in front of her. She noticed that her stepfather had asked for her favourites to be prepared and her heart twisted painfully. She and her stepfather had both tried to come to terms with one another, especially in the past two years, but they had never quite succeeded in reconciling what should have been a reasonable relationship. If nothing else, they both adored her mother and that should have bonded them, but it hadn't.

For his part, she suspected she reminded Lord Owain of her father. She had her papa's thick hair and his brown eyes, his reflexes in the training ring and his natural agility. There was no doubt in anyone's mind that Lord Owain adored his wife. She was the most beautiful woman in the castle—perhaps in the surrounding area—and that, coupled with her gentle nature, made her a prize to be treasured. But to be reminded daily that Lady Katherine had been married before, when she had clearly adored David Fletcher, must have been difficult for her stepfather, who worshipped his wife. But once Ari had tempered her behaviour and outwardly given up her intentions of becoming a warrior, he really had tried to connect with her. That his smiles never quite reached his eyes when he addressed her was something only Ari noticed.

But Ari would never give up her desire to become a warrior like her stepfather so desperately wanted. She had come up with several schemes to achieve her desire already, but they had come and gone before the answer had presented itself in the form of a betrothal to Lord Cradoc. Now the plan was very simple: convince everyone she was happy to be wed and escape on the journey. In the meantime, she had tried to make Lord Owain happy, if only to make her mother smile. She had done whatever he asked, behaved exactly as he wanted, but she was fairly sure her eyes didn't smile when she looked at him, either. The best that could be said for their relationship was that they were cordial and equally pleased to be parting ways tomorrow.

Sir Leopold's sleeve brushed against her arm and she jolted as the simple contact sent ripples of sensation skittering across her skin, bringing her back to the moment. His arm stretched out in front of her, reaching towards a dish. She noticed that light brown hair covered his muscled forearms, and that his palms were wide and strong. She wondered if they would fit around her waist…before shaking her head. Why on earth would she need to know that? There was no situation in which that would ever occur.

'Are you looking forward to your new life, Lady Arianwen?'

'Of course she is. Becoming chatelaine of her very own castle is what every woman aspires to.' Lord Owain answered for her and Ari's grip tightened on her knife, her knuckles turning white.

Just this meal left to go, she reminded herself and then she never had to see her stepfather again.

Never again would she allow someone to speak for her, to put words into her mouth that were not true.

'I am very much looking forward to the journey,' Ari said. It was the truth, after all. She risked a glance at Sir Leopold. He was looking down at her, a slight frown marring his forehead, his blue eyes hooded. Her own gaze fell to his lips and then flicked back up to his eyes. His frown had deepened, although she had no idea why.

Her mother struck up a conversation with her husband, and Lord Owain finally turned his attention away from Ari and the knight.

'Do I have something on my face?' Sir Leopold asked.

Heat poured over her skin again as she realised she was staring at him. 'Some crumbs,' she murmured, reaching up and brushing the imaginary bread from his beard.

It was his turn to jump at her touch and she snatched her hand back as if scolded. 'I didn't mean... I hope I didn't...'

What had she been thinking? She never normally went around touching the faces of men—or of anyone. She glanced at her hand as if to check whether someone else had taken control of its actions. But no, it still appeared to belong to her. Her face burned at her boldness and she was very glad that the Hall was lit only by candlelight. Hopefully, nobody else was witness to her strange behaviour.

'It's all right. I just wasn't expecting...' He shook his head. 'That's the problem with beards—they catch food.'

'I would imagine it comes in handy on long campaigns.'

His eyes blazed with amusement and a surge of triumph shot through her belly. She rarely made anyone laugh—not that she had many people to try to entertain anyway. 'Yes, I can always stow a loaf in there for later.' He pretended to pull an imaginary loaf of bread from the short hair on his face.

Laughter gurgled out of her, surprising her. Whenever she'd pictured her last night at Abertawe Castle, she'd imagined being too tense to pay any attention to her surroundings. But there was something arresting about Sir Leopold, something that took her out of the moment and transported her to a place where it was perfectly normal to notice the details of a man's face—the slight crease of a nearly hidden dimple, the long eyelashes and the dip in his top lip. Of course it wasn't, though. She'd never paid so much attention to the details of a man's face before. She could lie to herself and say that it was because she *had* to study him since he was her opponent, but that wasn't the whole truth. The reality was that she found him fascinating in an entirely new way.

They spoke then, although later, as she crawled into bed beside her sleeping sisters, she could not remember what about. The conversation had been easy, the laughter natural. It was a shame she was going to have to outwit him, but she was not going to change her plans merely because of a pleasant evening spent in his company.

She fell asleep almost immediately but woke to complete darkness. Her youngest sister was curled against her side, the weight oddly reassuring. Whatever relaxation Ari had felt during the feast had fled completely. She pushed her hair off her face, her fingers sticky with sweat. She was normally a good sleeper but tonight, when her freedom was so close, her heart was racing as if she was running. She wriggled slowly out from the tangled arms and legs of her sisters and made her way over to the window. She could only make out the blurry shape of the crescent moon through the mottled glass. She touched her fingertips to the pane, trying to ground herself. Slowly, her heart began to calm.

She was ready. She was prepared. Her plan would work.

She dropped her hands and headed back to her mattress. Tomorrow was the beginning of everything.

Chapter Four

Lady Arianwen was already mounted on her horse when Leo strode towards the stables. The early-morning sun caught on her braid, picking out ginger streaks amongst the dark strands, which burned brightly like flickers of fire. Leo swallowed as he made his way towards her.

It had been a mistake to engage Lady Arianwen in conversation during the evening repast the night before. Leo had tried to concentrate on what he was eating and on what Lord Owain was saying, but it had been almost impossible to tear his gaze away from Lady Arianwen or to stop himself from engaging with her. Now he knew that she was wittily observant, that laughter made her eyes crinkle at the corners and that her fingers were long and slender. Seeing her this morning was even worse. It was as if there were an invisible tie, drawing his eyes to her face, her long neck and her curves.

There was no one part of her that he could point to and say, *Yes, that's what makes her beautiful*. It was all of her, even the way she moved. Lady Arianwen was the essence of serenity sitting atop her mount. It was as if she had been shaped for this moment since birth.

He cursed under his breath; his own ludicrous thoughts

were going to make this journey harder than it needed to be. He had to hope that a few days in her company would dull his reaction because he could not afford to become a lovesick fool.

She was certainly not fighting an unwanted attraction to him. She barely even glanced at him. He didn't know if that made him feel better or worse. If she threw herself at him... His body stirred and he paused midstep. Hell, even thinking about her touching him had him hardening. He shook his head, moving forward once more.

Standing by Lady Arianwen's legs, Lady Katherine, her mother, was pressing her fingers to her eyes, as if trying to hold back the tears that flowed freely down her face. Tiny girls—who must be Lady Arianwen's younger sisters—stared up at their sibling, seemingly befuddled by what was going on. Only Lady Arianwen seemed confident and calm.

Leo strode closer, watching her the whole while. She had an excellent seat—better than most trained men he knew. She was perfectly balanced in the saddle, the reins relaxed in her hands. From a distance she gave every indication that she was a competent horsewoman, but up close there was a slight tremor in her fingers. It was the only sign that she was not as composed as she wanted to appear. He turned away from the sight. He didn't want to feel sorry for her, didn't want to contemplate what this journey might mean for her. He had to focus on his own goals, had to remind himself that it was imperative to prove he was not the failure his parents thought him just because he'd had the misfortune to be born second; and he must not let Tristan and Hugh down.

He must focus on the positives. If Lady Arianwen could

ride well, it meant the journey would be over quicker. The quicker they travelled, the earlier he could finish his mission and travel on to reach Tristan. There would be less time to spend gawking over his pretty companion, although the word *pretty* was doing her a disservice. It was too mild a word for what Lady Arianwen was. There was something otherworldly about her, something almost untouchable about her beauty that...

And he was doing it again—acting like he'd never seen a woman before. Thank goodness no one could read his mind because the old man from yesterday would not be the only one laughing at him. After years of not being attracted to any one woman, why was he interested in this one? Perhaps it was the very fact that she was forbidden to him that was so attractive?

'Are you ready?' Annoyance at himself made his tone more clipped than he intended and he winced. It was not her fault he had developed an inconvenient interest in her. He needed to remember that she was a gently bred young lady who was about to leave her home for the first time.

'Yes, Sir Leopold.'

He studied her expression. Her docile reply didn't quite match the twinkle in her eyes. Leo shivered as he threw himself onto Bosco's back. Beautiful he could handle— witty and amusing was going to be harder to resist.

'Then we should get moving,' he said to her. 'We have many leagues to travel today.'

'Lead the way, Sir Leopold.'

He glanced behind her. There was no activity from within the castle and nothing to suggest that anyone else was coming. However, he did not wish to offend anyone by being too hasty. 'Do you wish to wait for your father to say your farewells?'

Something flickered across her face, but it was gone before he could read it. 'We have already said everything we need to. There is no need to delay any further,' she said calmly.

He nudged Bosco into a slow trot. 'Very well.'

Lady Katherine started to cry harder as they began to move towards the gate. A younger daughter wrapped her arms around her mother's waist, which was the highest she could reach and, for the first time, Lady Arianwen's calm facade visibly cracked. She leaned over and clasped her mother's hands in hers and Leo brought his horse to a stop. It would be cruel to ride off now if Lady Arianwen had something further to say. 'All will be well, Mama. You will always be in my heart and I will think of you, here with my sisters, all the time. Please don't cry, Mama. I do not want my last memory of you to be a miserable one.'

Her mother wiped at her eyes. 'You're a good girl, Ari. I know the last few years have been hard on you but you have made me very proud. I know you will be a loving wife and mother.'

Another strange look crossed Lady Arianwen's face before her placid exterior was back in place. 'Thank you, Mama.' The hairs on the back of Leo's neck rose. That look, as fleeting as it was, set him on edge. There was something not right here, something that set his senses on high alert. Lord Ormand may have only taken interest in his trainees when they annoyed him but he had had some excellent instructors. One of Leo's favourites had been a man who had taught them how to read what a person's body and movements were communicating, and it was very clear here that Lady Arianwen's mouth was not saying the same thing as her body.

On the surface she was giving every impression of being a calm, young gentlewoman about to embark on her new life, but there were odd flashes of a hidden emotion, as if there was something going on that only she knew about. It could just be that the lady was nervous about the journey or about the marriage. Last night, during the feast, there had been an unspoken tension whenever Lord Cradoc's name had been mentioned, the odd word or phrase suggesting that Lady Arianwen's betrothed was a dour man. If Leo were in Lady Arianwen's place, he would be more than jittery. He would be rip-roaringly drunk and probably tied to the back of a horse because he wouldn't be going of his own free will. Not that he would ever find himself in that position because he had no intention of ever marrying. He planned to live and die on the battlefield. He was a warrior who'd never had any interest in the ridiculous courtly love that most knights indulged in. He believed it was a distraction from the main point of being a knight: the protection of the king and the country. And, if his one failed liaison had taught him anything, it was that he was not meant for relationships with women.

Or perhaps he was reading too much into this morning. It could be that *he* was apprehensive and he was projecting his emotion onto her. The muscles in his neck were so tight he felt they might snap if he got any tenser. That was probably what it was, but he couldn't be too careful. Nothing could upset his plans and so he would be extra vigilant, keeping a close eye on her until he could be certain that all was as it should be.

Leo circled around the yard on Bosco, allowing the women some privacy to say their final goodbyes. Lady Katherine only seemed to get more upset the longer Lady Arianwen tried to reassure her, clinging to her daughter's hand as if holding it would prevent the moment of departure. It was only when the younger children started to cry that Lady Katherine let go, seeming to calm down as she fussed over them instead of her eldest child. There was one last kiss, one last clasp, and then it was finally over. Leo bit back a sigh of relief as he led the way out of the keep, breathing more easily once they were out in the open and on their way.

Lady Arianwen made no comment as they wended their way through Abertawe. Every so often, his gaze would flick towards her despite stern words to himself not to do so. Her lips were pressed tightly together, the cords in her neck strained. He briefly wondered about offering to knead the stress away but quickly dismissed the idea. She was not a hunting dog who would lean into his touch, and this inexplicable desire to soothe her was absurd. There was nothing he could do for her, nothing… except… No! He was not going to let his mind wander in that direction. She was no more a damsel in distress than she was an animal in need of comfort. Rescuing her from her fate—if she even wanted to be rescued—was in exact opposition to his mission. No matter how lovely she looked or how her gaze made him feel, he could not deviate from his path. Too much was riding on his success.

He searched for something to say instead but nothing came to mind. Sweat beaded on his forehead and he wiped it away with his sleeve. Their ongoing silence was broken by merchants calling to one another in the winding streets that had built up around the castle, the smell of fish strong in the morning air. Overhead, seagulls called angrily to one another, racing to be the first ones to catch a haul from the local fishermen. Down below them, the wide bay looked better than it had when he'd arrived yesterday. The tide was in, covering the sludgy sand, and the bright blue water twinkled invitingly.

They turned to the east, squinting into the morning sun, and headed towards the river that fed the sea they kept on their right. It did not take long to reach the tall riverbanks of the Tawe where they turned inland. Leo rode ahead of Lady Arianwen to stop himself from gazing at her, listening for the sound of her horse's footfall rather than turning to check whether she was still with him. If he couldn't see her, he would be able to control his thoughts. One more glance and he knew he could lose control. If he saw her crying then he would have to comfort her, and if he had to comfort her then he might have to touch her, and that was not a good idea.

As time wore on, he realised his own self-protection was making him an insensitive brute. Lady Arianwen was without her family, probably for the first time ever, travelling with a man she didn't know, to a place she had never been to before. She was probably terrified. He should reassure her or, at the very least, put her at ease. He could converse on many topics, not just fighting or tactics. He, Hugh and Tristan were almost never silent. But the more he searched his mind for something to say, the less he seemed able to think of a single thing suitable for conversation with a woman. The silence became heavy, as if it were pressing down on him from a great height. Another league passed and his spine became rigid, the muscles tightening to an almost painful degree. He needed to say something, anything at all, to end the agonising quietness.

'Do you ever bathe in the sea?' he asked her when he was sure his nerves were about to snap his spine in half.

For a beat, she didn't answer. By the time he had convinced himself that she wasn't going to and that it was because he had just uttered the most boring comment in the last one hundred years, she said, 'The mud in the sand doesn't make bathing in the bay a pleasant experience. I found that out the hard way.' He turned to look at her and saw a small, wistful smile cross her face.

'How so?'

'The muddy sand is very slimy beneath the toes.' She pulled a face. 'Once I slipped in it and I was covered from head to toe. That was the last time I ventured in. The River Tawe, though—' she gestured to the wide river running alongside them '—on a hot day, is a good place to cool off.'

He turned away quickly in case she could read his thoughts from the expression on his face, because now he was picturing her, her undergarments clinging to her curves, as she climbed out of the water. He closed his eyes, trying to stop the images. It did not help. This was so unlike him. He did not fantasise about women. He had urges, yes, but he took care of those himself. It was easier, less complicated and had never once left him feeling dirty and used like his one encounter with a woman had.

'Is this the Tawe?' he asked. It was not his cleverest

comment, because he knew it was the Tawe, and even if he hadn't, what else could the large snake of water leading to the sea be?

'Yes,' she answered. 'It is.'

'Hmm, I thought as much.'

What! What was he saying? He was a better conversationalist than this!

He, Hugh and Tristan could talk for days or be in easy silence. Either way, it was never excruciating. And, although he didn't converse with women often, he had never had problems before. He felt like a fool and he had absolutely no idea why it was happening.

'Perhaps because Lord Owain told us to ride alongside it.'

His gaze slid towards her. Her lips were still pressed together but this time it looked as if she was holding back a smile. As he watched, she lost her battle with herself and a grin spread across her face. She turned and caught his eye and laughter burst out of her, the sound making him smile.

'Oh, dear,' she said when she finally stopped laughing. 'I do hope I haven't offended you. I don't know what was so funny about that.'

'It could be because it was a terrible attempt at conversation.'

She nodded. 'It was.'

He was about to point out that her uncontrolled laughter was probably a release of nerves but he held his tongue at the last moment. Now that she had laughed, some of the tension had left the lines of her body and he didn't want to bring it back.

'I'm normally better. I don't think, for instance, I have ever said anything so pointless before.'

She laughed again and the sound was like the sun coming out after days of rain. 'What would you talk about to your fellow knights?' she asked.

'Um…' He tilted his head to the side. 'Anything. Everything. Nothing that would be of interest to you.'

'Why don't you let me decide that?'

He scratched his chin. He didn't want to talk about the problems they'd faced recently, which was the topic that had dominated all their talk over the past month. He also didn't want to discuss his plans for his future because it didn't feel right, but that left his mind strangely blank. 'Swords. We talk about swords.' Did they? He couldn't remember but it seemed like something a maiden might believe a knight talked about a lot.

'Really? What about swords?'

'The quality.'

'I see.'

He glanced across at her again. Her eyes were shining as she looked at the path ahead. 'I fear you are laughing at me again.'

'Never.' But he didn't miss the way her shoulders shook.

'I speak the truth.' Now he was just talking nonsense but he was enjoying the way she was laughing, even if it was at him. He would keep going so long as she was entertained.

'Is the sword your weapon of choice?' she asked.

'It is.'

'What do you look for in a blade?'

'The quality of the metal used, the craftsmanship and the balance.'

She nodded thoughtfully. 'Does your current sword match these criteria?'

'It does.'

'May I see it?'

He leaned down and loosened it from its scabbard where it was tied to Bosco's side. He pulled it free, the familiar weight an extension of his arm.

'May I hold it?' Lady Arianwen was reaching out her hand as if she expected him to hand his blade over to her.

He barked out a laugh. 'What sort of knight would that make me if I handed my blade over to someone I barely know?'

'You don't trust me?'

Their gazes met and something hot and powerful simmered between them, something he *had* to ignore. 'I only trust two people and I am afraid you are not one of them. Not yet anyway.'

She dropped her hand, a look passing across her face. 'That seems fair enough.' She turned back to face the direction they were travelling, and he had the feeling he had passed some sort of test, one he'd had no idea he had been set.

He sheathed his sword and then leaned back in his saddle, allowing Lady Arianwen to pull ahead of him slightly. She really was a good rider, her slender frame swaying comfortably with her horse's gait. She pushed her hair away from her shoulders, pulling it away from the nape of her neck before allowing it to fall slowly back down. He realised he was staring and forced himself to look away, only to find his eyes pulled back. The urge to spur Bosco forward until he was closer, to lift her heavy strands of hair away and let them fall through his fingers, was almost overwhelming. He gripped his reins tighter and this time succeeded in tearing his gaze away.

He mustn't get distracted by the way she looked; it would be intensely foolish. He'd had a feeling that there was something not quite right about the way Lady Arianwen was acting and he needed to focus on that. She had tried to take his sword from him, and whether that was entirely innocent or something else he could not even begin to guess at, but he should be on his guard. Lady Arianwen may be exactly what she seemed—an innocent maiden on her way to her betrothed's castle— but if she wasn't, and if she somehow tricked or fooled him, then the shame would live with him for years. Not only would he let down his friends, he would also prove his parents right. He would be no better than the foolish spare they needed in case something happened to their superior firstborn.

They rode a little farther in silence as he stewed over the mystery of Lady Arianwen. He pondered leaving her to her thoughts but the farther they rode, the more curious he became. He pulled up alongside her once more. 'Are you well acquainted with your betrothed?'

'No,' she said with thin lips, and his unease fluttered in his chest once more. 'But I am sure he will make a comfortable husband,' she finished eventually.

He waited but she said nothing further. He would have to push if he wanted to find out more. 'That sounds like something you think you should say rather than the truth.'

She laughed softly and without humour. 'You're right, I suppose. There is not much I can do about my stepfather's choice of husband and so I hope that he will be

comfortable and if not… I will not be the first bride unhappy in her marriage. I will make the situation work.'

The resigned statement hit him harder than a passionate tirade. Here he was looking for double meanings in
her statements and perhaps all that was wrong was that
she was nervous. Hell, he would be if he were in her position. 'Does your father—?'

'Lord Owain ap Llewellyn is not my father,' she said
quietly but firmly.

'Ah, yes.' Leo shifted in his saddle. He was so awkward this morning, as if he had never made conversation with a woman before. Hell, as if he'd not spoken to a
person before. He wanted to give up and ride in silence,
and that desire was what pushed him to keep going. He
was the knight that fought on even in the face of defeat,
and he would not be thwarted by a simple case of awk-
wardness. 'Someone told me yesterday that your father
was the castle's master-at-arms. I am sorry to hear that
he passed.'

Lady Arianwen made a noise that he couldn't inter-
pret. 'I'm sure he would be proud of you now, on the way
to become the chatelaine of a grand castle.'

Lady Arianwen's snort of disgust was less hard to de-
cipher. He turned back to look at her; she was shaking
her head, a deep frown marring her forehead.

'You don't think so?' he asked.

'My father believed that noblewomen were lazy. He
would be very disappointed by how my life has turned
out.' Her brown eyes snapped to his, her gaze hitting him
in the chest almost like a physical blow. He turned away
before he got caught up in just looking at her. He had that
feeling again, the one that said to him that Lady Arian-

wen was not what she seemed, and he wanted to dwell on that, to think it through, but before he could his eyes were turning back to her. Whatever moment he thought he'd witnessed had passed and she was smiling gently as if he had imagined the whole thing. 'Of course, my stepfather only wants the best for me, and I am sure he has chosen wisely. I will endeavour to do my duty and bring honour to my family.'

Leo thought about his own mother. Although she wasn't the most loving of women—far from it—he could not deny that she was always inordinately busy. 'I don't think—'

'It doesn't matter,' Lady Arianwen said, the passion gone from her voice as if it had never been there. 'My stepfather is the head of my family now and I respect his choice of husband.'

Leo highly doubted the sincerity of her words, but he could find no more to say on the subject and they lapsed into silence once more.

She was intriguing, Lady Arianwen. One minute appearing to be one thing and the next there were flashes of someone entirely different. He must keep his wits about him, must look out for other moments where she might reveal something about herself.

Chapter Five

They rode in silence along the banks of the Tawe for the rest of the morning. Ari was content to let Sir Leopold lead the way, although she wished she didn't notice the way his hair was curling at the nape of his neck. It looked so soft, so at odds with the rest of him, which was all solid muscle and hard jawline. Her gaze kept falling to his arms; even in rest they looked powerful.

The stories of the way he rode seemed to be accurate. He and his horse moved as one, their combined size an intimidating threat to anyone riding towards them. He'd also had a perfect grip on his sword when he'd held it aloft for her to see. She was used to seeing the inferior grip practised by the current trainees at Abertawe Castle, as her father's replacement was not fit for the role he had. Neither of these actions she'd witnessed guaranteed that Sir Leopold was a superior knight, but they fitted with the tales about him and if they were accurate, then it followed that he was every bit as capable as he was purported to be. But none of this explained why he was in Wales escorting her to her betrothed.

She didn't want to engage with him, but each time they spoke she liked him more, and each time their gazes met it was harder for her to look away. She needed to keep to herself and maintain the distance between them. No good could come of getting to know him; no good at all.

'Why are you here?' she eventually blurted out when she could restrain herself no longer. She had held on as long as she had been able, and now the sun was high overhead. She bit her lip, but it was too late. She had already started yet another conversation.

He glanced about him, a small frown furrowing his brow. 'Um, because this is the way to—'

She couldn't help the laughter that gurgled out of her. He turned and smiled at her bemusedly, and her heart leapt in that irritating way it did whenever his attention turned to her. 'I don't mean here as in this stretch of pathway,' she clarified. 'I know that we are travelling towards Pembroke. I thought maybe you were here as some kind of punishment or trial. Otherwise, why would you be escorting someone like me across the country? Your seat is good and you can wield a sword—should you not be doing something far more heroic?'

His smile faded and he turned away from her as if focusing on the path ahead. 'You are a gentlewoman and—'

She rolled her eyes, even though he could no longer see her. 'I'm not really a lady, though, am I? Lord Owain ap Llewellyn is not my father, so I am a nobody. Before you protest, let me assure you that I'm not trying to charm you with false modesty. My father was a knight but he was not a nobleman, and my mother was born to an alehouse woman. If it were not for the fact that when my mother was widowed she caught the eye of Lord Owain, you and I would not be on this trip. I would have married some man from the lord's garrison years ago and probably already be on my fourth child.' Only she knew that this was not true, because she would have become a warrior instead since that had been her father's wish, but she wasn't going to tell Sir Leopold that. 'The nature of my birth is not a secret to anyone so what I cannot understand is why a knight of your alleged calibre is escorting someone like me to my future husband.'

He turned back to her, one eyebrow raised. 'Alleged?'

'All I have are rumours and tales to go on, so I am withholding my judgement until I see for myself what kind of man you are.'

He glanced about him. 'It seems we are out of luck. There are no ne'er-do-wells for me to demonstrate my prowess. You shall have to take my word for it that I can protect your honour if it comes to it.'

It was on the tip of her tongue to say that she could protect her own honour, but this time she managed to stop herself. It was odd that she was having to stop herself from blurting things out to Sir Leopold when she'd had years of practise at keeping everything she thought and felt suppressed. It was hard to tell if this was because she was so close to freedom that it was making her anxious or if it was something to do with him. Either way, she needed to be on her guard. She must not give him any hint that she was not exactly what she seemed because her plan to escape relied on him believing she was a sweet and delicate maiden with no way to protect herself. 'If tales of your prowess are true—' he grinned and her heart flipped '—you must admit that it is strange that you are here with me. I think there must be more to the tale.' She didn't miss the way his shoulders tensed as she spoke. She had hit a nerve and she wouldn't rest until she had found out the whole story. Perhaps there was something she could use to help her escape. 'Is there?'

He shifted in his saddle and Bosco snorted irritably. He patted the stallion's neck in apology and then let out a long sigh. 'There was an incident.'

'An incident?'

'I think I'd better start from the beginning.'

'Is it a long story?'

He shot her a look from his impossibly blue eyes. 'Do you have somewhere else you need to be?'

She smiled. 'I wasn't criticising. I was hoping for a lengthy tale. There's a lot of time to pass and I imagine staring at your back will become quite tiresome after a while.' Even as she said the words, she was not convinced they were true. Watching him move was endlessly fascinating.

His crooked half smile did strange things to her stomach—things she was going to ignore. 'Well, in that case, prepare to be entertained. But be warned, this is a sorry tale with an ending as sad as any Greek tragedy.' She grinned at his melodramatic tone, a near-perfect imitation of the bard who had regaled them in the Great Hall yesterday eve. He smiled back and her stomach flipped. Irritated with herself, she turned away from him. If she wasn't looking at him, it was easier to remain in control of her body. It was only when she glanced at him that things went awry.

'I'm the second son of Lord and Lady Beauvarlet.'

'Oh, well, if we're starting at your birth this tale really must take time to tell.'

'That fact is more for context.'

'I see. I've heard of the Beauvarlet family. Don't you own land in Kent?'

'I don't own any land at all but yes, my parents own a large swath in that area, which my older brother will inherit upon my father's death.' He cleared his throat. His horse jittered sideways, annoyed by the noise. 'Bosco,' Sir Leopold addressed his horse. 'You're very ornery today, old man.' The horse snorted in response. 'He's getting on in years,' he told Ari, 'and seems to find me more irritating as each day goes by.' The horse neighed as if agreeing with him and Ari laughed out loud. It was clear the horse and his master had a close bond and that Sir Leopold was teasing. The knight had a light manner, which she enjoyed and, in other circumstances, she would have liked to get to know him better.

'Anyway, to get back to my tale of woe.' Sir Leopold flashed her a grin and she couldn't help but smile back. 'My older brother, Alban, was sent to Windsor to be a squire and then a knight. I was sent to Lord Ormand's castle in Southampton. Have you ever heard of Ormand?'

She thought for a moment. 'No. Or perhaps yes. I am not sure.'

'That does not surprise me. Despite what Ormand thinks, he is far from the inner circle of the Crown. I am sure King Edward values his support in terms of the men Ormand supplies for his campaigns and the coin he has given to fund the war in France, but I digress… Where was I? Oh, yes, Alban is in Windsor while I am in Southampton, and I am…frustrated is the politest way I can describe it.'

'I see. So your older brother goes to Windsor, the seat of power of the English King, and you get sent to a backwater. Is that a reflection of your relative skill or the order of your and Alban's birth?'

Sir Leopold sighed, any trace of humour disappearing from his face. 'I guess that depends on whom you ask. My parents and brother would say skill.'

'But you would say it was because you were born second.'

'I would.' He nodded emphatically.

'Perhaps I think I have heard of Lord Ormand because travelling bards have spoken about your deeds. I presume his name would need to be mentioned in the tales. If it makes you feel any better, I have never heard tales of Sir Alban, if that is what he is called now.'

Sir Leopold nodded thoughtfully. 'I'm not sure how that makes me feel.'

'It should make you proud.' If people had heard tales of her skill with the sword, Ari knew she would not be able to stop rejoicing, older brother or not.

'It does but…it also angers me.'

'How so?'

'If I had been sent to Windsor, I hope that not only would you have heard my name but that I would have come to the attention of the king, or at the very least his most senior knight, Sir Benedictus. My ambition is to become one of the King's Knights.'

Ari whistled. The King's Knights were the most elite fighting force in the country. There were only four men in its ranks currently, and to gain admission was all but impossible.

'I know that is a challenging target,' said Sir Leopold, a tinge of red crossing his cheekbones, a pinkness that was adorably incongruous. 'But I think it is important to try for more.'

'I agree.'

'You do?'

'Yes. What is the point of never going beyond the limits that have been set for you? Of never making yourself uncomfortable in order to put yourself to the test? Life would be so dull if we never pushed ourselves to achieve more.'

He regarded her for a long moment and she feared she had given too much of herself away. What ambitions ought the lady of a castle have? Perhaps none, or perhaps none beyond honouring her husband and producing a pack of brats, but she would not be able to suggest anything else because she had never considered it for her own future, not once. 'You do not get on with your brother, then?' She couldn't imagine how she would feel if one of her siblings had the life she wanted, but she was fairly certain she would not be able to control her envy.

'How I feel about my family and our complicated relationship is not part of the story, but I would not say I do not get on with him. I barely know him.' There was more here, she was sure. She wanted to know but she dared not press. She did not want him to know her own thoughts and feelings so why should he tell her about his? 'As you can imagine, I didn't want to go to Ormand's castle. I believed I should be heading to Windsor, like my brother. On the day I arrived, bitter and sulking, I met two other boys in a similar situation to myself, Hugh and Tristan.'

'You became good friends?'

Sir Leopold half smiled. 'Not at first. I was determined to prove to everyone how wrong it was that I had been sent there. I worked hard to best all the other pages as quickly as possible. I'm sure I was insufferable. In fact, Tristan and Hugh never miss an opportunity to tell me that I was possibly the worst person they'd ever met outside of Ormand himself.'

He chuckled at the memory and Ari had to turn away. She had never had a friend to laugh with, had never experienced true companionship with anyone other than her father, and it had been so long since he had died that she sometimes forgot what his voice sounded like. Her mother's marriage to Lord Owain had elevated them beyond their former friends, but the higher ranked women of the castle had never really accepted her as one of their own. Perhaps if she'd had less interest in sword fighting she could have developed friendships, but she had been so busy hiding her real self and her ambitions from her mother and stepfather that she hadn't had time for other people. She'd been alone for years.

'What changed?' she asked. She had to keep the story going; she did not want to grow maudlin. Sadness never helped anyone.

'Ormand disliked Hugh and Tristan as much as he disliked me.'

'Why was that?'

'In the beginning, I think it was because we were children, and he doesn't really care for them. It's not until the pages become squires that he takes an interest in them, and by the time the three of us reached that stage we were able to beat him in any contest. Instead of being proud of his part in raising and training us, he was resentful that we were better than him.'

'How could he tell you were better?'

'Ah, good question. He would host a tournament every year in which he would compete with the squires. It was supposed to be a training exercise for us squires to learn what to do when fighting in years to come, but I think it was really to make him feel superior. It's a lot easier to best young men in tournaments than fully fledged knights, and he always won.'

'Until you?'

He grinned. 'Until us. He was not pleased, although of course he had to pretend that he was in order to save face.'

'How did you know it was a pretence?'

'Other than the glares and the pointed jibes at us, we were soon given all the worst jobs at the castle—polishing armour that was already gleaming, staying up in the freezing cold to watch for enemies that didn't exist, scrubbing out chamber pots.' He shrugged. 'You get the idea.'

Ari shuddered. She may not have enjoyed the restrictive life of a noblewoman but at least it hadn't involved chamber pots.

He flashed her a grin. 'Exactly. You can't hold yourself apart from two people when you're all retching into the same bush.' He chuckled softly. 'When I put my own bitterness aside, I realised there was something special about those two men—or boys as we were then. They have their own unique abilities, which makes us a fantastic team. We became as close as brothers.' He shook his head. 'No, that's not right. We are better than brothers. I would trust those two with my life whereas I wouldn't trust Alban with one of my shirts. After we became friends, we realised how well we worked with each other. Put the three of us in a training room and we are unbeatable. I am the quickest with the sword.'

'Modest, too,' she murmured and was rewarded with another grin. Annoyingly, her heart flipped over again. She bit back a sigh. She'd thought she was over that already and it was irritating that her body kept betraying her.

'Hugh is by far and away the cleverest man I have ever met, and Tristan, well, Tristan is devastatingly charming. Yes, he has the looks to help but he has a quick and clever tongue and can talk himself out of almost any situation.' Sir Leopold frowned. 'Nearly all, I should say.'

'How so?'

'If you met him, you would not need to ask.' His frown deepened. 'Actually, that would be a bad idea.' He stared off into the distance, appearing to have a sharp talk with himself, shaking his head as if his thoughts annoyed him.

'So what happened?' she prompted.

'Huh?'

'The three of you have become friends, despite your initial high-handedness.'

'I didn't say I was high-handed.'

His words sounded affronted but his eyes betrayed him. They twinkled mischievously and she fought her answering smile. She did not want to appear too amused or intrigued by him, although who was she trying to fool? 'Fine, despite your pig-headedness.'

He threw back his head and laughed, his Adam's

apple bobbing. 'Fine. I will admit that I was not at my finest when I first met my friends, but I improved and I know they would die for me now, as I would them.'

Sir Leopold stopped in his story and scratched his chin, the movement ruffling his short beard, which he smoothed back into place. 'This looks like a good spot to stop for a rest,' he said as they rounded a bend and came across a low bank that would allow the horses access to the quick-flowing river.

'You can't leave the story there.'

'I won't, but let's allow the horses to drink their fill and we can stop to have something to eat.'

Ari nodded. His suggestion made sense; she was very hungry now she stopped to think about it. She pulled her horse, Bel, to a stop, before slipping off and leading her to the river. Once the horses had drunk their fill of water, they led them over to a large oak tree. Allowing the horses to graze, the two of them sank to the ground, leaning against the rough bark of the tree. Sir Leopold may not have noticed but Ari could not help thinking how well they worked together, as if they had been following this routine for years.

The summer sun was warm, and the air around them buzzed with insects. Ari closed her eyes, allowing the stillness of the afternoon to seep into her bones. For the first time in a long time, perhaps ever, she was content. She was free from the constraints of her golden cage. She no longer had to worry about letting her mother down by causing her stepfather to frown disapprovingly. She could, to a certain extent, be herself, and the release was liberating as if she had broken free of her shackles.

It would be a few days before they had gone far enough

from Abertawe for her to make her escape. Too close to home and she would run the risk of being spotted by someone who might recognise her; too close to Lord Cradoc's castle and she might have left it too late. Midway was perfect. For now, she could relax and enjoy her time with this surprisingly entertaining man. She glanced across at him. His eyes were closed, his sandy hair loose around his face. He looked as handsome in repose as he did when he was talking, although she did enjoy the way his eyes sparkled when he was amused. And those arms... He was muscled in a way she had never seen before. Her fingers itched to trace the curves of his biceps, to sink her fingers into them to see if they were as firm as they looked. She tore her gaze away from them and back to his face. No good could come of thinking of Sir Leopold like that.

'Are you going to finish your tale?' she asked softly.

He opened his eyes, squinting against the sun. 'I told you that Tristan is charming but he is also very handsome.'

Ari raised her eyebrows.

Sir Leopold's lips quirked. They always seemed ready to smile, and she liked that about him. 'Both men and women seem unable to resist him, and Lord Ormand's wife and daughter were no different. Hugh and I helped him avoid them whenever we could, but we couldn't be with him all the time.'

'Lord Ormand caught him with one of them?'

'If only it were that simple. No.' Sir Leopold shook his head. 'That's unfair of me, and it makes it seem as though I am placing blame for what happened on Tristan, who did nothing wrong. Lord Ormand...' Sir Leopold stared out at the rushing river, a muscle ticking in his jaw. Ari doubted he was seeing the water as it hurried towards the bay at Abertawe. 'Lord Ormand was trying to ingratiate himself with the king. As a gift, he had a bible made. It took two years to complete and was inlaid with gold. It was a source of great pride to Lord Ormand, and he hoped it would buy his way into the king's inner circle.

'But the book was destroyed. There was considerable water damage and none of it could be saved. Tristan, Hugh and I are convinced it was Robert, a fellow squire, who did it in a fit of jealous rage, trying to frame us, but we have no proof and for obvious reasons we got the blame. As there was no evidence either way, we were not imprisoned but our punishment for our alleged crime was to be sent on a series of errands and denied the opportunity to try out for the group of elite knights at Windsor. It was a particularly cruel punishment because everyone knew how much the three of us wanted to go, how we are desperate to prove our worth to our families and to the leader of the King's Knights. Instead, we have been sent to Wales to...'

He didn't need to finish his sentence. Ari could understand how humiliating it must be for a knight of his calibre to be sent on such an errand. Escorting her to Lord Cradoc would bring him no honour, no glory and no opportunity to demonstrate his skill.

'Is your brother still at Windsor?'

Sir Leopold nodded briskly. 'He is.'

'And you feel you should be there?'

'It probably sounds shallow to you, but yes, I do feel as if I should be there.'

It sounded entirely reasonable to her. It was incredibly close to her own desire after all. 'Was there nothing you could do?' If she were him or one of his friends, she would fight with everything she had to get to where she wanted to be.

'I wrote to Sir Benedictus, the leader of the King's Knights I'm so keen to join. He also holds the highest position in the land, second only to the king. He is the king's most trusted adviser and all but rules the country in the king's absence.'

She was impressed. Not only was Sir Leopold literate, he was also confident and single-minded. He reminded her even more strongly of herself. In another life, they could have been kindred spirits.

'Did he reply?'

'He was more generous than I thought he would be. He told me there was nothing he could do about Lord Ormand's demands, but if we completed our missions successfully then he would consider us for his elite guard. To be one of his men, even if I never make it to the illustrious heights I dream of… To fight by the king's side is all I have ever wanted.'

Oh. Oh, dear. Ari's stomach twisted and she turned slightly away from Sir Leopold, unable to keep looking at his earnest face that was shining with hope. Sir Leopold would not succeed in his mission because she was not going to be delivered like a sack of potatoes to Lord Cradoc. They could not *both* succeed. She wasn't willing to sacrifice her own dreams, her own happiness. Not for a man she barely knew—not for anyone.

Chapter Six

They had been travelling for two days and nothing untoward had happened. Nothing in the physical sense at least. There had been no danger, no thieves or bandits in the woods, nothing to distract Leo from his travelling companion.

Every day they talked and laughed, and every day he was becoming increasingly captivated by the woman who was destined to become another man's wife. With each moment that passed it was becoming harder to imagine such a vibrant young beauty married to a dour old man—or indeed any man—without wanting to punch someone or something very hard. She was funny and brilliant and so beautiful it was sometimes hard to look at her. He cursed that this was the mission he had been assigned. It had seemed like the one most suited to his abilities but Hugh would have been better. His quiet, methodical approach would have afforded Lady Arianwen the protection she needed, but Leo knew Hugh would not have found her teasing humour to be as amusing or captivating as he did. Hugh would not have been in danger of engaging her in conversation just so he could see the mischievous twinkle in her eyes when she spoke, and

Tristan would have charmed her without getting caught up in her.

Tonight, he'd been relieved and disappointed when she had taken herself off to her chamber early. Relieved, because it gave him a moment to himself, a moment when he couldn't be distracted by her presence…and disappointed because it was her presence he craved.

He dropped his head into his hands. Perhaps he *was* the disappointment his parents believed. He was hot-headed and passionate, and he'd always thought these were good qualities. It was what made him fearless in battle, but now he realised it also made him dream of the impossible and that was not good. He knew she was a distraction, that he was less sharp than normal. These days riding through Wales had taken on a soft glow, almost as if they were bathed in summer sunshine. It was ridiculous because, even though it was summer, the Welsh weather was decidedly unpredictable and they had been covered in rain showers more than once.

The inn they'd stopped at for the night this evening was quiet. A low fire burned in the grate on the other side of the room. Two men were huddled in one corner, slumped in their chairs, muttering to one another over tankards of ale.

Taking a sip of ale, a creeping sense of wrongness settled over Leo. He ran his hands through his hair, trying to dispel the feeling of unease. This was surely his mind playing tricks on him, trying to conjure some reason to check on Lady Arianwen, to have another moment in her presence when such moments were nearly at an end. He took another sip of ale and glanced about him. There was nothing inappropriate here; there was no reason to disturb Lady Arianwen. He shook his head to clear his thoughts. He should finish his drink and get some rest. Tomorrow was another long day of trying and failing not to engage with his travelling companion.

He turned to observe the men in the corner. Perhaps his sense of disquiet was coming from them. They were doing nothing suspicious, but their slow murmur of conversation, which should be relaxing, somehow took on the form of a sinister incantation.

He took another sip. A log fell, sending sparks into the room. One of the men jumped, cursing loudly before settling himself. Leo smirked, half turning to share an amused smile with Lady Arianwen before realising she wasn't beside him. Lady Arianwen was safely in her chamber, probably sleeping by now.

He put his half-finished drink on the table and stood up, but nobody in the room spared him even the quickest of glances. It wouldn't hurt to check on Lady Arianwen, he told himself. It was nothing more than his duty, quite honestly. It would only take a moment of his time. It would reassure him that all was well with her, and the fact that he would get to see her smile one more time was not something he should dwell on. He took the steps two at a time, only pausing when he reached the door to her chamber, his hand hovering a hair's breadth from the wooden latch. He couldn't barge in. No woman would welcome an uninvited male storming into her space, especially if she was asleep. He would terrify her, and instead of her smile he could receive a blow to the stomach.

Taking a step closer, he pressed his ear to the rough wood. He could hear nothing—no one moving around, no soft snores, nothing. Perhaps she really was asleep.

He knocked lightly: nothing.

He knocked louder: still nothing.

'Lady Arianwen?' he called. 'Can you come to the door?'

Nothing. The hairs on the back of his neck stood to full attention. There should be some sound, something to indicate that Lady Arianwen was alive and well inside the chamber.

'Lady Arianwen, I'm concerned for your safety.' He forced his voice to remain calm even as his heart raced. 'I would be grateful if you could come to the door so that I can see you are well.'

The silence was long and palpable. The only noise he could hear was the pounding of his own blood in his ears. Something was not right, and the longer he stood here, the more certain he was.

To hell with it! If she was in a state of undress, he would have to deal with the consequences. He shoved the door open and strode into the chamber.

It was empty.

For a moment, the world stopped. Maybe he was in the wrong room but no, her bag—the one that held everything she was taking to her new home—rested at the foot of the bed. The chamber was otherwise tidy, the bedsheets undisturbed. Whatever had happened had occurred quickly and with little drama.

Don't panic, he told himself. *Any number of things could account for her absence. Perhaps she was hungry or wanted to stretch her legs.*

Even as he said the words, he knew none of these things was true. He had sat with her as she had eaten a hearty meal.

She was gone.

Why or how didn't matter right now. All that mattered was that he had failed, failed to protect her or failed to realise she was plotting to escape him. He'd been so caught up in their shared gazes, in the way she made him laugh and the long conversations they'd shared that he'd lost sight of what was happening in front of him. He'd let down his brothers in arms, proved his parents right in their estimation of him and allowed a young lady to come into danger. He was not worthy to call himself a knight, let alone one of the king's elite.

He turned and his eye caught on something snapping in the fire. He strode towards it. It looked like… He squatted to his haunches. It was hair, a thick coil of it smouldering in the embers. He would recognise the strands anywhere. He had dreamed of that hair, of wrapping it around his fist and—

He swallowed. He reached out to touch it, snatching his hand back at the last minute. He didn't need to burn his fingers to know what was before him. Wherever she was, Lady Arianwen no longer had her long locks. He surged to his feet, the need to find her even greater than before. Why would anyone cut off such beautiful hair?

There was only one way to know: find her.

Ari had no idea how long she had been travelling. The moon had long since disappeared behind a thick cloud and there was no sign of an impending dawn. Her head dropped to her chest and she forced herself to sit upright. Beneath her, Bel trudged wearily. They were both going to have to rest soon, a necessity for which she foolishly hadn't planned. But neither she nor Bel could go much farther without stopping. They both needed rest before they continued. She'd always been so excited by the possibility of freedom that she'd imagined herself possessing endless, boundless energy. The reality was far from that. She was exhausted, but even if she hadn't been, Bel was.

A breeze rustled the trees overhead, sending a chill down her back where her long hair had so recently been. She reached up and touched the roughly chopped ends. She'd always planned to cut her braid off—she could not pass as a male warrior if she had a woman's hairstyle. She'd cut through it with her dagger, the sharp blade slipping easily through the strands. Tears had pricked the backs of her eyes as she'd stared at the long coil in her hand, the pang of sadness taking her by surprise. This was something she'd planned for and it was a simple enough action, but the wave of grief was real and immediate. Perhaps she should not have been surprised. Although a straightforward deed, it was symbolic of the end of one life and the beginning of another.

As she'd held the thick braid, she'd remembered the way her mama's comb had slid through it, those intimate moments a time for the two of them to connect. Then came an even older memory of her papa comparing the colour to his own, the pride evident in his voice. Throwing it on the fire had felt like a betrayal of her parents, particularly her mother, which was illogical, because this whole expedition went against what Lady Katherine wanted for her future. When Ari's stepfather had prohibited Ari's training, it had been obvious that her mother was relieved. She hadn't wanted her daughter to follow masculine pursuits and when Ari's betrothal had been arranged, she had been thrilled that her daughter was making such a good match. Ari had known then that she would have to deceive her mother because she had no intention of ever marrying Lord Cradoc. But Ari still loved her mother and it had hurt that it was increasingly clear that she was not and never would be the daughter her mother wanted. But Ari would not throw her life away to satisfy someone else's dream, or to make her mother happy. Even so, seeing the shorn braid had hit her hard. It was so final; there was no going back now.

She slipped out of the inn easily, the sight of the magnificent Bosco the only thing that had made her pause. She'd pictured Bosco's rider sitting astride the large mount, his gaze full of laughter, and her chest had tightened. She had never thought she would come to like her escort, had never imagined for a moment that her leaving him would cause her pain. In what should have been a joyous moment, she knew that she would always regret sneaking away in the middle of the night and not saying goodbye to someone who had become, if not a friend, then at least someone important to her. That she had sacrificed his future for her own did not feel good, either.

Ari brought Bel to a stop and slipped gratefully to the ground. Her eyes were almost accustomed to the dark now and she could make out a break in the treeline that ran along the path she had been following. Tugging Bel, she moved in between the trunks, stopping when she was a reasonable distance from the rough track. The temptation to sink to the ground and rest her eyes pulled on her but she resisted the urge. Instead, she saw to Bel, loosening her light load. Only when she was sure Bel was satisfied did she lower herself to the ground, resting her back against the rough bark of a large oak tree. She pulled her cloak tighter around her; she had underestimated just how cold it was going to be at night, and the material did little to stop the cool night's breeze cutting through to her skin. She shivered. Tucking her cloak around her neck, she sank lower to the ground, trying to shield herself.

She felt her eyes flutter closed. She would just rest them for a moment and then she would keep going. She had much ground to cover before morning.

When she awoke, she was airborne. She blinked a few times, trying to make sense of what was happening to her. Somehow—and she couldn't fathom how—the ground was moving below her as she swung from a height. She blinked again. She appeared to be slung over a wide shoulder, arms clamped tightly around her waist and legs. Panic bubbled through her, but she managed to clamp her lips shut. She didn't want to make any sound to alert her abductor that she was now awake. She'd been so far away from the path—how had this person found her? But wait, she recognised the red surcoat and the broad shoulders—they were as familiar to her as her own. She had spent the better part of two days gazing at them whenever she'd had a moment, somehow memorising the way they flexed and rolled.

It could mean only one thing: Sir Leopold was here.

Her heart skipped a beat as if giddy with the happiness of seeing him before steadying with a dreadful thump. Her body might be pleased to see him again but it was purely a physical reaction. Mentally, she was devastated. She could not be caught as quickly as she had left.

She'd known he would chase after her, had known that dodging him would be a challenge, but she had believed herself capable of eluding him. It had never occurred to her that she would get caught within hours of escaping.

She squirmed and his arms tightened even harder around her. She kicked out, connecting with a rock-hard stomach.

'You can kick as much as you want to,' Sir Leopold growled, his words vibrating through her stomach. 'I'm not going to let you go.'

His anger fuelled her own. 'Put me down!'

'No.'

'You don't know what you're doing!' He was ruining everything, taking away the freedom she had longed for, for so long. This was her only chance.

'I know exactly what I'm doing. It is you who have lost complete control of your mind.' One of his arms moved down her legs and she gasped as his warm hands curled around the skin of her calves. It was as if he were branding her with his touch. She wriggled, trying to free herself from his hold, but he only tightened his grip.

The woodland floor was passing quickly by. Before long they would be back on the track and she would never get away from him there. She forced herself to go floppy, relaxing in his hold. He grunted and shifted her weight, which was exactly what she wanted. She twisted and threw herself to the side. It caught him off balance and he let go of her. She tumbled to the ground, landing awkwardly on her side.

'What are you doing?' hissed Sir Leopold, grabbing for her.

She dodged his outstretched hand, rolling away. He

grunted and lunged for her again, but she was too quick. She staggered to her feet. For a moment, they stared at each other, breathing heavily. There was so much she wanted to say but there was no time: she turned and ran.

Dawn was starting to break through the leafy canopy, lending everything a soft glow. Despite the extra light, it was hard to make out the twisted roots of the floor below. Ari stumbled over the uneven ground but she was still moving quickly. Behind her, Sir Leopold cursed as he crashed after her. She weaved in and out of the trees, not following any particular path, changing direction every few paces so as to make it harder to follow her.

'Stop!' he yelled.

She ignored him. She risked a glance backwards. She wasn't getting away from him but he was still not upon her; there was still a chance she could get away. She dodged around a large tree. Farther ahead of her was a denser patch of trees with plenty of undergrowth. She had to get inside it and then—

Strong arms clamped around her waist and she was pulled tightly against a solid chest. She struggled, twisting and turning in the firm grip, but it was no use. She may as well have been in an iron cage for the impact she was having.

He held her, not saying anything, until she finally stopped moving. Her chest tightened as she realised that she now had no hope of escape from him. He was as strong as he looked and she could not overpower him, not without a weapon. She was well and truly beaten and he had barely even had to try.

Gradually, their breathing calmed, but neither of them moved. Her awareness of their surroundings gradually penetrated her consciousness—the cacophony of the dawn chorus, the rustling of the leaves overhead, the warmth of his body. His arms loosened their hold a fraction but she didn't step away. She could argue it was because she knew he would catch her easily but the truth wasn't as straightforward. He may have been her captor but he was also the man whose arms she had been yearning to touch. She should be running or pleading with him to let her go, but she remained still. His hand moved down her back, adjusting his hold perhaps, but the touch sent spirals of something rushing through her. She shifted, moving closer, pressing against him, and he grunted softly, sounding almost pained. Now she was here, in the circle of his arms, and it was almost as if this space was made exactly for her. Fragments of thoughts chased each other through her mind, images of running, the brush of lips against hers, an urgency for something she couldn't name. None of it made sense.

'Come on,' he murmured gently. 'We need to get back to the horses.'

Keeping one arm slung over her shoulder, he began to lead her in the direction they had just come. Baffled by her tumbling thoughts, Ari allowed herself to be tugged along.

Sir Leopold stopped at the edge of the woodland and gazed down at her, his eyes full of sympathy. Her heart fluttered oddly. She'd expected him to be furious. She'd run from him, kicked out at him, tried to ruin his all-important mission, and yet his expression was kind. The urge to say something, anything, to him pressed on her but she held herself still, forcing herself to remain silent.

She was not in her right mind in this moment. Anything she said would reveal more of herself than was wise.

'I know what it's like,' he said eventually, 'to have a path thrust upon you, one you didn't choose.' She nodded slightly, her heart expanding with hope and maybe something more, an emotion she could not quite name. No one had ever truly seen her, nor tried to understand what she was thinking. 'I can only guess what it must be like to be made to marry someone you don't know. But…your stepfather has given his word that you will marry this man and, hard though I'm sure it is to imagine, I'm sure you will eventually find contentment in your new situation.'

As he talked, the fluttery sensation died away to be replaced by a hard knot of anger. Her thoughts finally began to clear. To compare their situations was outrageous. Sir Leopold was still a knight, even if losing her would mean he would not be considered for the King's Knights. It may take him longer than he'd originally planned to achieve his goals, and his career may not be as illustrious as he hoped but he would be free, free to choose, free to roam the country, free to fight whenever he pleased. Their scenarios were not even remotely comparable. Her stepfather had already stripped her life of everything she enjoyed doing, and her future contained only the promise of misery.

'You know nothing of how I feel!' Her response burst out of her.

He stepped backwards, his eyes widening at the force of her indignation. 'Then tell me. Perhaps I can help.'

His calm reply only stoked the flames of fury higher.

'If I tell you, will you let me go? Will you let me make my own way in life?'

He inhaled deeply before letting it out slowly. 'No.'

Her fists tightened. 'Then there is nothing you can do to help me.' Sir Leopold may offer her platitudes, may claim to be able to understand her but in the end, he was like everyone else. And why should he put her happiness above his own when she would not do the same for him? A heavy weight settled in her stomach. She hadn't truly expected him to be willing to help her, but the confirmation that he was like everyone else hit her hard, almost as hard as her capture, a capture she could not yet wrap her head around. This could not be the end for her; it could not be her only chance to get away. It would be harder now that Sir Leopold knew of her desire to get away, but she could not bring herself to accept a future in which she must marry Lord Cradoc. That small sliver of belief was the only thing keeping her from dropping to her knees in utter despair.

He seemed to take her silence to mean that they had finished talking. He turned and stepped out of the treeline, leading her with him. They both squinted as the bright morning sunlight hit their eyes. The horses whickered in greeting and Ari realised just how deeply asleep she had been. She'd slept through her horse being moved from her side to a path some distance away from where they had stopped.

Sir Leopold vaulted onto Bosco, watching her intently as she climbed onto Bel. He needn't have worried. She did not have a hope of getting away from him while they were both on horseback. Bel was quick but she was no match for Sir Leopold's magnificent stallion.

'Why did you cut it off?' he asked, gesturing to her hair.

She reached up to touch the ends. 'I...'

She didn't want to tell him how she planned to live as a man but she had no other explanation to give him. Even if she hinted at the truth, it would reveal too much to this man who would do everything in his power to thwart her plan. Oh, she trusted him with her safety; he'd never hurt her physically. She'd been fairly sure of that before tonight's escapade, but now she was certain. Even with her trying her hardest to fight him, he had not retaliated. But she couldn't trust him with her secrets; in fact, she trusted no one.

She dropped her hand. 'It seemed like a good idea.'

He stared at it for a beat longer, his expression unreadable. 'I suppose it must be heavy to carry around.'

She nodded. It wasn't the reason she had cut it but his comment was true nevertheless.

'It was.'

He leaned over, his knee brushing against hers, his hand risen as if he was about to feel the blunt ends. She tensed, unsure how she felt about him touching her in such a way, but he dropped his hand and turned away from her as if the moment had not happened.

'Let's go.'

He waited until she pulled ahead of him, before following closely behind.

The journey back to the inn seemed ridiculously short. During the lonely night she thought she had travelled many leagues, but it was perhaps two at the most. She was sagging with exhaustion by the time they stabled their horses, the tiredness stripping away her anger. She stumbled over some uneven ground and his arm came around her, catching her before she crumpled to the floor. This time, he wasn't holding her to keep her from getting away and the difference, for her at least, was astonishing. She felt the contact down the length of her body, and her skin sparked to life, sensation running all over her. He smelled delicious—of wood and soft leather. She hadn't noticed that when they were fighting in the forest. Without thinking, she leaned against him and inhaled deeply. He stiffened and she reared back quickly. She blamed tiredness for her reaction, because she would never normally go around smelling people.

'Let's eat,' he muttered, guiding her across the small courtyard. She was more grateful than she would ever admit for his supporting hand under her elbow.

In the taproom, he led her over to a small fire and left her there to warm her feet while he spoke to the inn-keeper. He returned with two steaming bowls of stew and a couple of tankards of ale. She ate the first few spoon-fuls so quickly that she didn't even taste it. It wasn't until she caught his amused gaze that she slowed down, taking her time to savour the meal between mouthfuls. She hadn't thought enough about food in her escape plan and her stomach felt empty despite not missing out on any meals yet. She had some dried meat packed in her bag and money to buy further food along the way, but she now realised that was inadequate. It was better to find out now than several days into her solo journey. The next stop on their trip would be at a larger town. She would have to find a way to purchase more food once they were there.

The ale was far tastier than she'd expected from such

a small inn. Sir Leopold replaced her first one with another and this time she savoured the sweet liquid.

'Why did you run away?' he asked softly as she came to the end of her second tankard.

Maybe it was the utter tiredness sweeping through her or the two ales she'd had, but Ari suddenly found she wanted to spill to Sir Leopold the secrets she'd kept for so long. She stared into the bottom of her tankard. She must not tell him, no matter how sympathetic and caring he seemed. He would not support her when he realised that success for one would come at the cost of the failure for the other. She had to remember that, despite his soft voice, he would never give up his dream for hers.

She looked up at him. His blue eyes were so expressive, and right now they were filled with compassion. The words just tumbled out of her mouth, definitely helped by the sweet beer. 'I don't want to marry Lord Cradoc.' It was strange saying the words out loud after keeping them inside for so long. It was as if she'd been carrying a stack of logs around for a long time and was finally able to put the burden down. She felt lighter, lighter than she had for years.

He nodded, seemingly unsurprised by her answer. 'Arranged marriages are difficult but they can work. My parents are a good example of this. They didn't meet before their wedding day and they work well together.'

'I thought you didn't like your parents.' He'd said that, hadn't he?

He frowned. 'I never said anything like that.'

'It was implied by your tale. The one where your parents sent your brother to Windsor and you to an insignificant castle on the south coast.' She knew she wouldn't much care for her parents had they treated her like that.

But Sir Leopold was shaking his head. 'That doesn't mean I don't like them. I have great respect for them, which I am sure they will return when I join the King's Knights.'

Ari frowned. Sir Leopold didn't seem as confident as normal. His words rang with the sound of a phrase often repeated but not necessarily believed. '*Respect* doesn't necessarily mean *like*.'

'It's the same thing.'

Arianwen respected her stepfather, he treated her mother and sisters well and was a competent lord of the castle he ruled, but that did not mean she liked him. 'Are you sure you can change your parents' minds? In my limited experience, once someone has made up their mind about you, it is very hard to change their opinion.' Impossible, she would say. She had never managed to get her stepfather to see her as anything other than an irritant, no matter how hard either of them had tried to get past their initial dislike. It was highly unlikely that anything Sir Leopold did would change his relationship with his parents. He could become the King of England but if they had decided his older brother was more entitled to their admiration, then that was the way it would always be.

But Sir Leopold was shaking his head. 'You do not know my parents. Besides, this is not what we were talking about. I was saying that although my parents' marriage was arranged, it has worked well over the years.'

'It's not that I don't want to marry Lord Cradoc specifically,' she said instead. 'It's that I don't want to marry at all.'

He straightened, his eyes widening. 'You want to join a nunnery?'

'If that is my only other option,' she said, turning away from him so that she could no longer meet his gaze. Those eyes of his could get her to say more than she wanted.

'Is it that you want to marry someone else?' There was something urgent in his voice, a tone she had not heard before.

'No.'

If she hadn't been keenly aware of him, she would have missed the slight loosening of his shoulders. He picked up her tankard and poured some of his ale into her empty one. She raised an eyebrow and he shrugged. 'You seem to like it more than I do. It's too sweet.'

'There's no such thing as too sweet,' she countered, taking another sip of the ale. It was absolutely delicious. 'Are you trying to get me drunk?' The taproom had taken on a slightly fuzzy edge that hadn't been apparent when they had first arrived, but she was fairly sure she still had her wits about her. If he thought more alcohol would get her to spill her secrets, he was very much mistaken.

His lips twitched. 'Of course not, although I am interested in why you are so against marriage if it is not a nunnery or another man making you feel that way.'

She took a sip of ale as she mulled over her response. There was no reason not to tell him why she didn't like the idea of marrying; it had no bearing on her plan. 'My father married my mother for love and they were ridiculously happy together.' She waved her hand around in the air as if this somehow encompassed all that had passed between her mother and father. 'Sometimes it was hard to be in the same place as them because they were always cooing over each other.'

'Yes, I can see how that is an awful example of marriage.' Sir Leopold smoothed his beard, his eyes twinkling, and she couldn't help it—she was back to staring into their depths.

She couldn't stop herself smiling back at him. 'Their marriage was lovely but…my mother is a soft and gentle person. She is easy to love and I am…' She stopped before she told him that she was a warrior, that her life was for fighting and that she was not cut out for married life. 'I am not.'

He was already shaking his head. 'You are very easy to—'

He shook his head again. Was it her imagination or were the tips of his ears turning pink? She squinted but the light was too dim to be sure.

'I am sure that Lord Cradoc will adore you. You are funny and clever and…' He waved his hand around in her general direction. 'You have nothing to worry about.' A strange warmth curled in the pit of her stomach. She glanced down at her tankard. She had nearly finished his portion of ale, too. That must be the reason for the sensation. It could not be linked to Sir Leopold's comments. They fell well short of a declaration of love—it was faint praise, if anything, and it would be pathetic to be pleased by his words.

'We can agree to disagree on that,' she said quickly. 'Anyway, my father died.' She took a deep breath, the horror of his passing as fresh today as it had been all those years ago. Her mother's screams as his breathing had slowly come to an end echoed in her ears. She pictured the chasm that had opened up in their lives, then the one that had been filled, at least for her mother, by another man. When she was sure she had herself under control, she continued. 'As you know, my mother remarried, this time to the Lord of Abertawe Castle. It was a brilliant match for her as it secured our future. We had a place to live and we never went hungry.'

'Again, this is hardly the diatribe against marriage I was expecting.'

'I'm coming to it,' she said. 'My mother is a very sweet, kind woman and I know that Lord Owain has been a good husband to her. He does not beat her, he provides for her and for me, he gives her every luxury she wants, and she now has a brood of children that she always wanted.'

'I am still not sure this scenario gives the bad impression of marriage you seem to be—'

'She didn't have a choice,' Ari burst out. 'She loved my father and within a year of his death she was married to someone else with a babe on the way. Without my father to provide for us, we had no way of supporting ourselves. We would have been out of the castle and goodness knows where if she had not tied herself to Lord Owain. She *had* to marry because there was no other option.'

'Is she unhappy?' he asked gently, all traces of humour gone from his face.

'She wouldn't tell me if she was. She wants everyone to be happy and she knows that it would upset me if I thought she was not content. But I have seen her in love and I know that is not what she feels for Lord Owain.

She is bound in a marriage, a marriage from which she can never escape, because there was no option for her to choose something different.'

Sir Leopold leaned back in his chair. 'There are different kinds of love. She may not be as passionate about Lord Owain as she was about your father, but if she has given no indication that she is unhappy with the arrangement then perhaps she is as content as she seems.'

He was beginning to irritate her now. He was entirely missing her point, and, despite the amount of ale she had consumed, she was sure she was arguing her case well. No one should have to marry if they did not want to. In her case, she did not want to marry because she wanted a different type of life, but even if she had wanted a husband, Lord Cradoc would not be the man she would choose. 'Are you planning to get married?' she asked, trying a different tack.

He pulled a face. 'No. Never.'

'Aha!' She waved a slightly wobbly finger at him. 'And why is that?'

'I intend to spend my life on the battlefield. I would barely see a wife.'

'There are many men who live like that. Some wives might even prefer it.'

He laughed. 'Now *that* is not a ringing endorsement of marriage. A woman would only want to be married to me because she won't see me very often.'

His eyes were twinkling again and Ari didn't think he'd taken real offence, but it still irritated her that he was not understanding what she was trying to say. 'If it was an arranged marriage then it's possible your bride would be happy to send you off to battle, but of course you could marry for love.'

It was his turn to snort. '*That* will not happen.'

'Why not?'

'Because…' His gaze dropped to her lips before returning to her eyes. The air around them stilled. He swallowed, and something hot and heavy burned inside her. He cleared his throat, rubbing his chest and dropping his gaze to the tabletop. 'It will not happen because… women and I do not mix.'

She frowned. 'We're mixing.'

He raised an eyebrow. 'Not in the sense to which I am referring.'

Heat rushed up her spine as she caught his meaning. This time, there was no doubting the images that flooded her mind. Sir Leopold, his long fingers tracing the length of her jaw, the brush of his beard against the soft skin of her neck, the length of his body as it pressed against hers. An answering heat flickered in his eyes and she leaned towards him, something else controlling her movements, something wild and primitive. He mirrored her movements until she could feel his breath against her cheek.

He straightened in his chair, his gaze shuttering off as if it had never burned for her.

'Now, if you've finished that drink, I think it is time we both slept. We have a long way to travel today and it will be easier if we have rested.'

She snapped herself upright, dizzy at the speed with which the conversation had changed. The moment had been thick and heavy with potential, but maybe she had imagined it because he was nothing but brisk and cold now. Or maybe it was because she was exhausted. She was tired—more so than she had ever been before. She staggered to her feet, thinking of nothing but the welcoming mattress upstairs. Later, after she'd slept, she could begin to make sense of everything that had passed.

Chapter Seven

The River Twyi turned towards the west in a wide curve that seemed to last forever, until finally the high grey walls of Carmarthen Castle came into view.

'It's not far now,' he murmured, stating the obvious but desperate to have some sort of communication with Lady Arianwen. She had not spoken much to him after they had risen yesterday. They'd not travelled far, having wasted so much time during the night before, and had spent the night in the smallest settlement he had ever visited. It had been cramped and smelly but at least it had meant he and Arianwen had been forced to sleep in the same hall as the other residents, meaning it had been impossible for her to escape, and that had been a torture in itself. To lie so close to her and not be able to reach out and pull her closer, especially as he now knew how she felt in his arms. He'd held her twice now, and each time it had been more difficult to let her go. She fitted perfectly against him, as if he had been born to hold her and only her. And, when he had held her, well, it had done things to his body, things he hadn't realised he'd been capable of feeling. He'd wanted nothing more than to slide his fingers into her hair and press his mouth to hers. She'd probably have hit him if he'd attempted such a thing and so he was glad he had held back. He didn't want to make this experience any worse for the two of them than it had to be. This journey was certainly a lesson in restraint. If he had given in to his desire, she would have slept in the cage of his arms, and he would have told himself it was to keep her from escaping because that was the only acceptable excuse.

'I'll be glad of a rest. I am very hungry.'

Lady Arianwen seemed to be making an effort to return their relationship to what it had been like before her escape attempt, and yet so far neither of them had quite made it work. Leo glanced sideways at Arianwen, his heart giving that strange lurch that only the sight of her seemed to cause. It was worse now with her short hair. Somehow, the shorn locks emphasised the angles of her face, throwing her beauty into stark relief. It was irksome how his gaze sought her out so often, as if she were a temptation put on earth to test *him* specifically, to lure him away from his chosen path. She wanted to escape from her marriage and damn him if he didn't want to help her. He wouldn't. He couldn't. And yet…

'I have some oatcakes,' he said, to stop his mind wandering into very dangerous territory. He leaned backwards and reached into his saddlebag and pulled out a couple. 'Here.' He held them out to her. She took them from him, her fingers brushing his as she did so. His hand tingled long after she had begun to eat.

'Would you like one?' She held one of the biscuits out to him.

He shook his head. 'I am not that hungry.' His appetite had not returned since he had found Lady Arianwen's chamber empty. Right now, she was placid and polite but he had no doubt she was going to try to escape again, and he would have to stop her, no matter how much sympathy he felt for her. If somehow the worst happened and she did manage to outmanoeuvre him, then his life would be over. He would not be able to face his friends because he would have let them down spectacularly. He would never be able to face his parents, who would learn not only of his original disgrace, but also that he had failed to make it right. He shuddered as he pictured his father's face—a mask of utter disgust for the failure of his second son, the one he didn't really want and whom he believed had never lived up to the Beauvarlet family name.

But that was not all of it. There had been moments yesterday when desire, hot and potent, had almost been his undoing. The worst had been at the inn when she was soft and sleepy, full of sweet ale and staring at his mouth as if she wanted nothing more than to reach across the table and touch her lips to his. And he had wanted to, so badly it had almost hurt not to do so. And yet this was a line neither of them should cross. If they began to develop feelings for one another, this whole impossible situation would be even harder for them both.

Bosco snorted irritably, not keen on the way Leo was pulling so firmly on his reins. He ran his hand along his horse's neck, reassuring the beast that his master was not going to give in to his passionate nature.

'I cannot betray my brothers.'

'I'm afraid I did not hear that. What did you say?'

He swallowed; he hadn't realised he'd spoken out loud. 'I was thinking of Hugh and Tristan. I hadn't meant to speak.' He wondered what they would say about Arianwen and the predicament in which they found themselves. Hugh would think about it from every angle and would probably advise Leo to continue on the path that led towards successful completion of the mission. To do otherwise would be a betrayal of the agreement Leo had made with Lord Owain, and Hugh always followed the rules.

'Are you missing them?' asked Arianwen.

'I...'

Did he miss them? He wasn't sure. He should, they were always together but...

His thoughts were entirely consumed with Arianwen—the way she laughed, the way she teased him mercilessly, the way she was so desperate to escape that she would risk her life to do so. 'I'd like to ask their opinion.' That much was true. Hugh, in particular, had always been able to stop Leo from doing something rash and impulsive.

'On what?'

'On whether I should have let you escape when you attempted it.' Perhaps he shouldn't be so honest with her, but it was more important to him than it should be that she knew he was not heartless. Hell, he wanted to help her. If she didn't want to get married to a man old enough to be her father, she shouldn't have to but...he had given his word that he would deliver Lady Arianwen to her betrothed, and to do otherwise would mean that he was too passionate and impulsive to control his actions. It would also betray his friends. He couldn't do it, and every time the stray thought crossed his mind in the future, he would need to crush it down.

'What do you think they would say?' she asked quietly, and he hated the faint thread of hope he could hear in her voice, hated it because he knew he would destroy it.

'Hugh would tell me I did the right thing.' He heard her quiet grunt of dismay and winced. 'Promises have been made and they must be upheld.' He waited for her to say something but the response to that was nothing but the sound of the horses' hooves on the dust track. 'Tristan would probably agree to that, too.'

'You don't sound so sure about that.'

He scratched his head. 'Not for the reason you think. He would agree with Hugh and me—' Leo needed to stress to her and remind himself that he should stick to his mission's goal '—that promises must be kept, however… He would probably be able to charm you into thinking going to Lord Cradoc's was exactly what you wanted.'

'Impossible,' she snapped.

He glanced across at her. She was frowning fiercely, glaring at the walls of Carmarthen Castle as if she could incinerate them with her look. Fool that he was, he wanted her to direct that look at him. There was something so intense about it, so fierce. He let out a long breath. He was in serious trouble if he wanted a woman to scowl at him. Serious, serious trouble.

'You haven't met Tristan yet. He can charm anyone.'

'No man could charm me into changing my mind about this.'

'Very well. Perhaps he would charm Lord Cradoc into thinking that he does not want you to be his wife.'

Arianwen slowed her horse and looked at him speculatively. 'Perhaps we should go and get this Tristan.'

Leo grimaced. He'd been making light of the situation, not thinking that his words would cause her to hope for something that would never happen. 'I'm afraid that will not be possible. Tristan is engaged on his own mission and he cannot be found until it is over.' It was a lie but a necessary one.

His chest tightened as she slumped in her saddle. It hurt him to see her so sad, although why it made him feel so awful, he wasn't sure. The thought that he was causing her pain and misery was horrendous to him; he was desperate to see her smile again. He knew he should spend some time thinking about why her sadness was making him feel this way, but he had a feeling he wouldn't like the answer and so he refused to dwell on it.

He supposed he could give her some reprieve. Perhaps he could allow her a day at Carmarthen, some time to wander around the market. It would be one of her last days of real freedom before her marriage. He shut down the voice that told him this was foolishness, and was for his own benefit and not hers, because *he* wanted to spend more time with *her* before their real lives began.

Before he could talk himself out of it, he said, 'I think we should spend the day in Carmarthen tomorrow.'

She said nothing. He tugged at his collar, which was becoming uncomfortably tight.

'It will give the horses a chance to rest.' His was a palfrey. The stallion could go for days without stopping and both horses had already rested enough yesterday. Leo was floundering now, saying more than he should so that she didn't guess he wanted to pause in their journey so he could spend more time talking to her. 'And for us to stock up on supplies.' That was the work of half a morning, if that. She still wasn't talking and so he stopped. If he rambled on further, he was in danger of blurting out something that revealed just how much she was coming to mean to him.

Bel skittered sideways and Arianwen rubbed her neck, muttering soothing words that Leo could not make out. 'Your idea to stay the day...' she said eventually. 'I would...like that very much.'

It was another league before he realised he was smiling, and that it was a smile of true happiness. He tried to suppress it; it was not for him to be happy or sad about today. This was about giving Arianwen more time to be free before her marriage. But every time he thought he had his face under control, his smile slipped back into place.

Leo liked Carmarthen on sight. The small town had a warm feeling about it, as if the very streets themselves were welcoming them. The guard at the gate gave them directions to an inn deep within the castle walls, and the two of them led their horses through the rabbit warren of narrow lanes. It turned out to be an excellent recommendation. The scent of roasting meat filled the taproom, and the landlord and his wife were effusive in their welcome.

'We have a chamber upstairs or you can stay in the barn with the horses,' the lady said, handing them a fresh roll without them having to ask. The bread was still warm and Leo found himself watching the joy on Arianwen's face as she bit into it rather than answer the question. Her eyes took on a dreamy look as she chewed, and he couldn't tear his gaze away.

She swallowed. 'Do I have something on my face?'

'Mmm…a crumb.' He reached up and brushed the soft skin of her cheek. Wiping away the imaginary grain, he remembered the night they had met when she had reached across and gently touched his face. The sparks that had shot through him then should have been a warning for him to get far away from her, but he hadn't, and now here they were with him touching her face and wanting, more than anything, never to let go.

She held still, her brown eyes looking up at him. There was no reason for him to keep touching her and yet he could not pull away. His thumb brushed the length of her jaw, dropping to her neck where her pulse beat as wildly as his.

'The chamber, sir?' prompted the landlady, her lips turned up in a knowing smile.

Leo leapt backwards, dropping his hand as heat flooded his face. He'd been all but stroking Arianwen— No, he *had* been stroking her, as if he had the right to touch her as he pleased. All this talk of not giving in to his impulsive side and he kept failing. If he kept giving in to his baser desires then he would be unsuccessful in his mission, just as his parents would expect him to.

He straightened. 'We'll take both, please. The lady will have the chamber upstairs and I will sleep with the horses.' He had absolutely no plan to spend the night sleeping amongst the livestock. He might be dazed by Arianwen's otherworldly beauty but that didn't mean he had completely lost his wits. He was going to spend the night outside her door to ensure she didn't try to escape again, or if she did, there would be no late-night tromp through the woodland because he would catch her before she even left the inn. He was sympathetic to her plight but not a fool.

'Do you want a moment to refresh yourself before we head out?' he asked her.

'Yes. I won't be long.'

He followed her slowly up the stairs and leaned against the wall opposite her chamber door. Just because she had made her escape attempt at night last time did not mean she would do the same again. If she knew how towns like this operated, then she would know that the gates in the walls surrounding the town would shut at sunset, and she wouldn't be able to leave after that. Daytime was her best opportunity here.

Her door was already closed by the time he reached the top of the stairs. Inside, he heard her bag drop to the ground and her footsteps as she moved about. She didn't keep him waiting long. He heard her walking towards the door but he did not move away to hide that he had been waiting for her. He wanted her to know that he would be watching her every move. She gave a start, her eyelids fluttering with surprise as she stepped out.

'What are you doing?'

'That should be obvious. I'm ensuring you don't use this as an opportunity to slip away from my watch.'

The faint flush across her skin betrayed her. He smirked at her, glad she realised how closely he would be keeping an eye on her. She lifted her chin and swept past him, the very essence of wounded innocence. He grinned at her back, before following her downstairs.

'Is there anything you would like to buy?' he asked as they stepped into the warm summer air.

'Bread and oatcakes for the days ahead perhaps,' she suggested. 'Do you have coins?'

'Yes, your father gave me some for the journey.'

'*Step*father,' she corrected.

'You are very keen to make that distinction. Do you not have a good relationship with your fa—with your mother's husband?' He suspected that the answer was no from everything she had hinted at, but he was interested to hear her story.

She shrugged. 'We get on well enough.'

'That doesn't answer the question.'

She smiled sadly. 'I told you, he is very kind to my mother and looks after her as if she were a precious jewel. He has given me lovely sisters whom I adore and provided me with a home. To begrudge him his care would not speak well of me.'

'And yet you do.'

She flinched but didn't deny it. 'I think he was hoping for a different sort of stepdaughter to the one he got. My mother is very... Well, you saw her. She is an incredibly beautiful. She is also accommodating and sweet. I think Lord Owain thought I would be the same and was disappointed to discover I have a mind and desires of my own. For my part, I was frustrated that he wanted me to be someone I am not. Words were spoken early on in their marriage, words that neither of us can forget no matter how hard we try.'

'What words?'

She stopped in the middle of the street and turned to him. Her gaze was frank and assessing and not at all docile. He was glad; he'd wanted to see the real her.

For all the good it would do him...

'You are very persistent,' she said. Normally he wasn't, but she was a mystery he wanted to unravel. 'It's not something I really want to talk about. Like I told you, Lord Owain has performed his role as stepfather to the best of his ability. It's… We didn't always see eye to eye, that's all.' She turned towards the street that was lined with merchant shops. 'Shall we see what treats the baker has for sale?'

He wasn't done questioning her but he was realistic enough to realise she would not reveal more at present.

Chapter Eight

Arianwen looked around her, orienting herself on the long narrow streets, planning a route to the gate that marked the only way through the thick stone walls that lined the town. Next to her strode the hulking great warrior knight, the man who was the current obstacle in her chosen path and who was currently occupying far more of her thoughts than he should be. She told herself that she *had* to think about him because she needed to escape him, a feat that was going to be far harder than she'd anticipated, but that wasn't all that was on her mind.

She peered up at him. Instead of looking for potential weak points in the fortifications, she found herself noticing that the beard she had always thought of as light brown had a patch of blond, just below his left ear. Her fingers twitched with the urge to run them through it; it shouldn't matter to her how soft it might feel and yet, for the better part of a street, it consumed every thought.

Her gaze dropped to his shoulders. Two nights ago, he had held her in the circle of his arms. Yes, that had been to stop her escaping but she was sure it wasn't her imagination that, before he had let her go, it had turned into something else. Something potent, something that had come back to her in hot fragments while she slept.

He cleared his throat and her gaze darted to his face. He was watching her, grinning.

'I'm studying for weaknesses,' she said before she could feel awkward for being caught staring at his muscles.

'You won't find any.'

She rolled her eyes heavenward. 'You're very confident.'

'With good reason.' His lips were twitching, ready to break into his easy grin.

'You always seem about to smile,' she commented. 'I've never met anyone else like that. You seem happy, even though your future is on the line and you know that I am going to do everything I can to escape this marriage.'

His smile faded slowly. 'I didn't know you were going to try that hard but I appreciate the forewarning. However,' he said, his grin returning to full force, 'I'd be a strange man if I didn't appreciate someone admiring my muscles.'

She snorted. 'I wasn't admiring them.' Of course she had been.

'Yes, you were, and I don't blame you. They are impressive.' He flexed his arm, the bulge of his biceps appearing through his clothing.

She couldn't help her laughter bursting out of her. It was easy to forget that this likeable, amusing man was her opponent, and he was a force to be reckoned with. She'd managed to get away from him easily enough that first attempt, but he had found her quickly. He must have considerable tracking skills to locate her in the dark with nothing to give away her position. She wanted to find out how so that she could cover her tracks next time, but Sir Leopold also appeared to be clever and asking would probably give away her intentions. Perhaps a bit of flattery would work.

'Fine, they are admirable.' He smirked; perhaps her adulation needed finesse. She had never tried to charm anyone before. 'You are obviously very skilled as a knight.'

'Oh, I am.'

The levity in his voice suggested he wasn't taking her compliments seriously, but she pressed on; she might not have another opportunity to question him. 'You found me very quickly the other night. Were you taught tracking skills as part of your training or is it a natural ability?'

'It was…' He paused. 'Oh, that was very nicely done, my lady. I was almost about to tell you how I found you.'

She clenched her fist. Was it only moments ago that she had been thinking of how thoughtful and considerate he was? He was beyond annoying. 'I don't know what you're talking about,' she tried lightly.

His laughter boomed around the narrow street, somehow slipping beneath her ribs and catching her breath. 'My tracking skills are part of my extremely excellent natural talent,' he said when his merriment finally died down. 'Let's leave it at that.'

They carried on in silence for a while. Ari had no idea what Sir Leopold was thinking but she was entertaining herself with visions of pushing him into the River Twyi, and if that also included him getting out with his wet clothes clinging to his impressive muscles, only she needed to know that.

They finally came to a stop outside a bakery, the smell of fresh bread making her stomach growl despite having eaten back at the inn. Sir Leopold stood with his hand stroking his beard as he looked at the queue ahead of them. She wondered what it would be like to touch the hairs on his face. Would they be soft or would they prickle? Her fingers itched with the desire to find out. Her feelings about this man were never consistent. One moment she wanted to do him mild bodily harm; the next she was desperate to touch him. No one had ever made her experience such contrary emotions. What was it about this man that did?

'What are you frowning about?'

She hadn't realised that he'd turned to look at her. His eyes glinted with amusement and her skin heated. She could hardly tell him the truth. He might let her find out and then she would be lost because he would know the power he seemed to have over her.

'I'm very hungry.'

'Ah, me, too. Shall we?'

He indicated the stall behind him. Her gaze roamed over the assorted goods covering the table. If she was honest, she wanted it all—the flaky pies, the crisp loaves…everything. 'Some oatcakes,' she said. These would travel well, they wouldn't crumble and they would last for days, unlike the bread, which she desperately wanted to shove into her mouth.

He nodded before asking for them and handing over the required coins when told of the price. 'What's this?' he asked the baker, pointing at one of the loaves she had been eyeing intensely.

The baker's chest puffed out. 'It's one of my bestsellers, a special recipe of my own design. A bread made with honey. It's sticky and sweet. I can highly recommend it to you and your wife.'

Ari flinched at the mistaken assumption, but Sir Leopold did not miss a beat. 'I'll have some of that, too. A couple, if you please.'

The baker handed over their goods and wished them good day.

They took a few steps away before Sir Leopold came to a stop. 'This is for you.' He handed over a large chunk of the honeyed bread. 'I noticed you enjoy sweet things.'

'That is very kind of you,' she said, taking the bread from him and trying not to appear too eager but desperate to taste it. She took a giant mouthful and nearly groaned. Above her, she heard a quick inhale but when she glanced up at him, his face was impassive. She took another bite; the bread was the most exquisite thing she had ever eaten. 'When did you notice that about me?' she asked after she'd swallowed. They had not eaten anything like this since the journey had begun.

'When you nearly inhaled your sweetened ale and then mine. It gave me a hint.' He grinned, his eyes dancing, and her stomach squirmed, which had nothing to do with the bread.

'I never did such a thing,' she protested.

'Hmm, just like you're not trying to make your mouth bigger so you can fit all of that in.'

She grinned around her mouthful. It was true. She was trying to force in as much as possible, but who could blame her? This was the loveliest bread she had ever tasted.

'Would you like some?' She held the bun up to him.

'And deprive you of a morsel?' He shook his head. 'I'd rather take my chances with a stray dog.'

She burst out laughing. 'I'm not that bad.'

'You can't see yourself,' he teased. 'Which is just as well…'

She put the last chunk in her mouth, licking her fingers when she'd finished, unashamed of her reaction. He wouldn't have bought it for her if he didn't want her to enjoy it. 'You should try the one you bought for yourself. I've never tasted anything so good.'

He smiled and her stomach flipped oddly. What on earth was happening to her? First, it was her heart jumping all over the place, and now it was her stomach that wouldn't stay settled. Every time it was something to do with him. 'I would, but I'm keeping it for later, and I can't buy any more because my coins are for something else.'

'What do you need?' she asked.

'I'd like to see if I can get myself a new blade.'

She fell into step beside him as they continued on their walk through the town. 'What type of blade are you looking for?'

'A new dagger. Something light but strong.'

'What happened to your old one?'

A shadow crossed his face. She didn't like to see him upset, which was ridiculous because her future actions would devastate him. 'It was taken from me.'

'I cannot believe someone like you would let that happen.'

He raised an eyebrow. 'Someone like me?'

She gestured to his broad chest and muscled arms. 'You were the one harping on about your muscles. Surely you're far too strong for someone to get the better of you.'

He smiled before his eyes turned dark again. 'I thank you for your faith in me but this was a different type of taking.' He glanced down the length of the street and she had the feeling he was not seeing the cramped row of shops in front of them. 'The dagger was given to me by Lord Ormand when I started my training. He took it away as part of my punishment for the manuscript being destroyed.' They walked on a few paces, and Ari searched for something to say in sympathy but came up short. 'I could have refused, I suppose,' he continued. 'But I think that would have made my situation worse. I could have been ejected from his household and service altogether if I showed any sign of disobedience. I think that was what Lord Ormand was hoping for but I defied him by staying calm.' He turned to her, one eyebrow risen. 'And that was an incredible achievement for me, just so you know.'

Ari couldn't imagine a worse fate for Sir Leopold than to be denied becoming a knight at all. She knew what that was like because being refused something she desperately wanted was the life she was living. She also knew how devastated she would be if someone took away her blade. It had been a gift from her father and it was her most treasured possession—it was her only true possession, in fact, but that was beside the point. She was slowly coming to realise that she and Sir Leopold were cut from the same cloth. It was a shame he would never know it. When she had escaped from him, he would hate her for ruining his chance of succeeding on this mission.

Sir Leopold stopped to ask for directions and she watched him as he spoke. He was respectful and attentive and her heart squeezed. To stay with him and reach their destination would give him the life that he wanted and she was beginning to want that for him, too. But she couldn't do it at a cost of her own future. She'd lived for so long in the shadows, biding her time, waiting for her chance, that she could not give it up, not for anyone, and yet...

She tore her gaze away from him, frightened at the path her thoughts were following. To even consider, for the briefest of moments, giving up everything for a man she barely knew was preposterous. Sir Leopold knew she did not want to marry Lord Cradoc and he was not offering her the same courtesy. He had made it very clear that he intended to get her to Pembroke, even knowing how she felt about the upcoming marriage.

No matter how she was coming to think of him, she could not allow herself to be turned from her mission. In a few days, she would never see Sir Leopold again. Whatever the outcome of this journey, however he felt, however she felt...it was all irrelevant. She cleared her mind of thoughts of him and began adding to the map in her mind, laying out the formations of the street and calculating the best way to navigate the labyrinth of tightly packed buildings.

She was quiet as she followed him the rest of the way to the blacksmith's; engaging in conversation with him was only making her like him more.

Unfortunately for her resolve, *he* did not remain silent. 'That man told me the best one in the town is round this corner. This is the blacksmith whom the Lord of Carmarthen uses so he must be good.'

She wanted to protect herself, she really did, but she

also loved to talk about weapons and couldn't help but ask him questions as she followed him along the route.

She remembered their conversation about swords from the beginning of the journey, about how it was his weapon of choice. It was her preferred weapon, too— another thing they had in common. 'What is it about the sword you enjoy so much?'

'In all combat it is you against your opponent, both of you warring for dominance. But with the sword, you are up close to your foe. You can look into his eyes and see the moment you are going to win because it has dawned on them that you are the better swordsman. It's not just about your respective skill with the blade, either. It is also a battle of wits, trying to predict what move your adversary will make and counter it, calculating how soon it will be before he tires, and what manoeuvre you can perform that will take advantage of his weaknesses. There's nothing like it.' Ari blinked; these were her thoughts exactly. Sir Leopold had just described what she loved so much about combatting with a sword, almost as if he had reached into her mind and plucked the words from her head.

'How are you with a bow?'

'Not as good, but I'm a fair shot.'

'What would be your average range?'

He shrugged. 'From here to there, I suppose.' He gestured an impressively long distance away. She searched his face; he did not seem to be teasing her so he was probably being truthful. He was good, then, far, far better than any of the men at Lord Owain's castle. And if he was better with the sword than that…well, she had to hope she never got in a fight against him.

The smithy was at the end of a long row of shops that abutted the town walls on one side. It looked very different from the one at Abertawe Castle, which was the only other one she had ever come across. There, the blacksmith's workshop was sheltered from the elements by a roof, but the sides were left open to allow the heat of the furnace to escape. She had always enjoyed walking across the courtyard to the rhythmic clink of metal on metal as the blacksmith shaped and tempered the weapons. The sound reminded her of her father, who'd had very exacting standards when it came to blades and who had taught her to be just as precise in her requirements.

This blacksmith's looked like a shop from the outside, encased on every side with a wall. She and Sir Leopold stepped inside and Ari staggered backwards as they were met with a wall of fierce heat. Sir Leopold raised a questioning eyebrow and she shook her head, indicating that they could carry on.

If she was going to live as a warrior she would have to visit a blacksmith by herself, and she wanted it to appear as if it was something she did all the time. It was good to get the experience in now. Next time she entered one that was enclosed like this, she would be prepared.

They moved farther into the room, the heat settling against her skin like a thick blanket. A man hammered metal that had a glowing tip and for a long moment, she and Sir Leopold watched, mesmerised. Eventually, the blacksmith finished. He lifted his head and looked at them, both eyes astonishingly white in his smoke-stained face. 'How can I help you, sir?'

Sir Leopold stepped closer. 'I'm looking for a dagger and I hear you are the man who can supply me with the best one in town.'

The man's chest puffed out, proud of the praise. 'Aye, I believe I can. Do you want one made specially or would you like to see what I have in store?'

'While I'd love to commission one, I need to move on quickly. I would value seeing what you already have.'

'Very well.' The blacksmith nodded.

The two men moved deeper into the shop, Ari stepped back towards the exit, taking care to study the way the street curved so she did not make the mistake of travelling down it later. It wouldn't do to get caught up in a dead end. She would not have long before sunset and the closing of the gates, and she would need to be quick.

She was so busy committing the buildings to memory that she didn't pay attention to the approach of a new man until he was very close to her, too close.

'You're a pretty little thing,' said the newcomer, leering down at her.

Ari sneered at the man. She'd been called *a thing* before and she hated it. No one had ever made the mistake of doing it twice.

'Short hair on a woman is unusual but it means I can see more of your pretty face.' The man reached across as if he was about to touch the ends of her hair, but she slapped his hand out of the way before he could connect with the strands.

His lips twisted into an angry scowl. 'How dare you!'

He made to lunge towards her and she braced herself to deliver a counter-attack, but before the man could move, a large hand appeared on his shoulder, holding him in place. Over the man's head she could see Sir Leopold, his face a mask of icy rage. Sir Leopold yanked the man away from her as if he were removing a flea.

'Griffiths,' said the blacksmith, moving towards them, wiping his hands on his apron. 'I told you, you're banned from my shop. Now get out of here before my new friend here throws you into the gutter where you belong.'

'I don't think so,' growled Griffiths, his face turning an unhealthy shade of purple. 'After all the business I've given you over the years, you will not treat me with such disrespect! I've come for the blade I ordered and you'll give it to me now.'

Ari was impressed by Griffiths's audacity. Even with Sir Leopold holding him in place and growling in his ear, he still had the effrontery to act as if he was in charge of the situation.

The blacksmith shook his head. 'You haven't paid me for anything I've given you over the last year. I may have been a fool before, believing in your lies, but I will not compound that by giving you another thing. Now get out.'

'I've got another proposition for you,' the man sneered. 'Give me what I ask for, and the woman, and I'll not burn your place to the ground.'

Sir Leopold snarled, and the next thing any of them knew, Griffiths was flying through the air, landing on the cobblestones outside with a thud. Sir Leopold followed him out, still snarling. Griffiths got to his feet, his fists curled, but whatever he saw on Sir Leopold's face caused him to turn and run.

'That man is a menace. He's more than rich enough to pay his bills but his position as constable to Lord Carmarthen gives him a false sense of his own entitlement. He hasn't paid me for some time,' the blacksmith commented as Sir Leopold stood glaring at Griffiths's fleeing form. 'Not many men stand up to Griffiths. Your husband is impressive.'

'Yes,' Ari murmured, her gaze fixed on the warrior whose strength had touched something deep within her. 'He is.'

Chapter Nine

Leo placed the dagger on the table between him and Arianwen and admired the way the metal glinted in the candlelight. He and Arianwen had returned to the inn to eat and, although it was still light outside, the windowless taproom was dark save for the light given off by candles and the fire. It was cold, too, with no hint of the summer's warmth making it through the thick walls.

'You're very pleased with it, aren't you?' He glanced up at Arianwen, who was smiling at him, the warmth in her eyes settling in his stomach like a fine mead. He didn't even sigh over the now familiar lurch his heart gave whenever he looked at her.

'I am.' The blacksmith had given him a superior blade at a hefty discount after he had seen off the unfortunate Griffiths. Leo would never admit, not even under the threat of death, that his rage had not been directed at the man's inability to pay for goods he had been provided with, but at the insolent way Griffiths had spoken to Arianwen. When he saw the cur reaching up to touch her, the anger he had felt eclipsed anything he had experienced before. He knew he would have killed Griffiths if he had hurt her even a small amount, and the knowledge that he'd have such a strong reaction frightened him.

'May I?' Arianwen asked, holding out her hand for the knife.

'Of course.' He picked it up and passed it over, his fingers brushing hers as he did so. 'What would your father have thought of it, as a man-at-arms?'

She shot him a look, her lips parting. He bunched his hands together to stop himself from threading his fingers through her hair and pulling her towards him so that he could press a kiss to her mouth. Urges like that were coming often now. That, coupled with his earlier anger, was making him question everything, everything that he didn't want to doubt, because his life was already planned out and it did not involve putting those plans in jeopardy to help a woman he had only just met.

He watched as Arianwen balanced the knife on a fingertip. 'The weight is perfect.' In a move he could barely follow, she flipped it until she was holding the handle. 'The grip is excellent.' She held the blade to the light. 'The edge is sharp.' She twisted it round so the handle was facing him. 'My father would have allowed any of his men to carry such a weapon.'

He paused for a beat, staring at her over the proffered dagger. Slowly, he took it from her, never breaking eye contact, feeling every thump of his heart like a heavy blow against his rib cage. His fingers brushed against her wrist and his pulse began to race. She had assessed his blade as if she had been born for it, moving it far more smoothly and precisely than he could.

In that moment, he knew he could fall in love with Arianwen. She was funny, smart and adept. Her interest in weaponry and the discussion they'd enjoyed about it this afternoon had been one of the most interesting conversations he'd had in a long while. It was a tragedy that she was promised to someone else and that his very future, and that of his brothers in arms, depended on his delivering her to that person. If he had met her under any other circumstances, he would have stopped at nothing to make her his. To think that he had found someone who made him feel like this, after years of believing he never would, was nothing short of a miracle. But the situation wasn't different. It was exactly what it was and there was nothing he could do to change it, not without consequences that would change the course of his life.

He pocketed the knife and turned his attention to the fire hoping, rather than expecting, that the sight of the flames would take his mind off the woman sitting opposite him. It was a futile expectation; thoughts of Arianwen were beginning to consume him, to take over every waking moment.

'I think I shall retire.'

He looked up. Arianwen was stretching her arms in the totally unconvincing manner of someone who was preparing for a long night's sleep. The wretch was clearly planning to try to escape again. Unsure as to whether he was amused or frustrated, he forced himself to show no reaction. It wouldn't do to tell her how obvious she was or how entertaining he found her. If she ever succeeded in escaping from Lord Cradoc, Leo would have to hope she didn't join a travelling band of actors because her performance was shockingly terrible. 'Very well. Shall I escort you to your chamber?'

Arianwen shook her head. 'No. I am more than capable of walking up a small staircase and opening a door by myself.'

He grinned, forgetting all about his longing for what he could not have. Even though he knew it was foolish and it was giving in to his impulsive nature, he was looking forward to seeing what she had planned for tonight. By rights, he should tie her to the bedpost and be done with it and yet he found he couldn't do it. That made him weak, he knew that, and once again he didn't want to think about his motivations too deeply. He only knew that the thought of taking her wrist and binding it tightly so that she couldn't move made his stomach roil with nausea. 'I know you are capable of opening a door but I will still escort you. I suggest we set out early in the morning. We have much ground to cover.'

A slight grimace crossed her face and he instantly felt guilty about teasing her. Flummoxed, he didn't know what to say and, without waiting for him to add anything, she turned and made her way upstairs.

'Hell,' he muttered as he got up to follow her. He'd ruined the end of what had been an almost perfect afternoon. What he wouldn't give for a tiny slice of Tristan's natural charm. This situation was painful for her and, like a fool, he had just made light of it.

Ahead of him, Arianwen's feet pounded the wooden stairs, every stomp reverberating around the narrow space. The corridor leading to the chamber was only just wide enough for him to walk through, his shoulders brushing against the walls. 'You realise I'm not leaving you alone?' he murmured as her hand reached for the door handle. She turned back to face him. Even in the dim light given off by a nearby candle, he could still make out her long eyelashes as she blinked up at him.

'You can't come into the chamber with me,' she said firmly.

'I can and I will.'

'But—'

'But what?' He leaned down to hear her speak, their faces so close now that he could smell the faint trace of the lavender soap she liked to use. Desire coiled in his stomach, hot and primeval, obliterating his common sense. Her lips parted and he lost control. He bent his head and touched his lips to hers. Everything, his whole world, centred on where their bodies touched.

Which was the only explanation he could give for what happened next.

Hands shoved against his chest, momentarily knocking him off balance. Before he could react, Arianwen was inside the chamber and a key was snicking in the lock.

He stared at the doorway for a moment, shaking his head at his own carelessness. Once again, he'd given in to his impulses and this was what had happened.

'Unbelievable,' he muttered.

He shoved against the closed door. It was the work of only a few moments to break the lock, but in that time Arianwen had already managed to clamber out the tiny window, an opening through which he would never fit no matter how hard he tried. He strode over to it, calling her name. She stopped and gazed up at him from the street. It was a reversal of their first sight of one another, and time seemed to stretch and slow as he looked down at her. Once again, he couldn't seem to break the gaze, despite the urgency. And then she was turning and running.

He cursed viciously before racing down the stairs and out into the street. There was no sign of her, but he knew where she was heading and she would not get away from him that easily.

Chapter Ten

Ari clutched her small bag to her chest. She had brought virtually nothing with her, just her food and some rations and her dagger strapped to her thigh, so she didn't have to rummage through her bag to get to it. Her coins were sown into her clothes and now that she had made the hard decision to leave Bel where she was, she did not have to carry provisions for the horse as well. As much as it would have been easier to travel with Bel, retrieving her from the stables would have taken up valuable time.

From the way the sun was almost dipping below the castle walls, she knew she did not have long before the gates were shut and she was trapped within. Her chest was tight and she knew it was not from the speed at which she was moving, but from guilt. Sir Leopold had kissed her and she'd pushed him away, using his momentary distraction to her advantage. But instead of triumph, she felt sick to her stomach. The feather-light touch of his mouth on hers had almost been enough to wipe her purpose from her mind. Her body had screamed at her to pull him closer, to find out exactly what it felt like to have his mouth plunder hers, but she had forced herself to hold on to a tiny fragment of reality. This might be her last chance, and she'd had to take it, even though it hurt to do it.

She risked a glance behind her. She could see no sign of being followed, although she knew Sir Leopold would not be far behind. Her knees trembled slightly at the thought of him capturing her. Not only would he be angry that she had run away from him again, but he probably wasn't thrilled by her behaviour in the corridor, either. She just had to be quicker than him and then she would never have to find out.

Another narrow street completed and the gate was getting closer. Not long now and she would be free. The streets were quiet as the residents settled down for the evening, those who were out paid no attention to her as she hurried along.

'Hey!' a voice called out to her as she passed a tavern but she ignored the summons. She knew no one here and someone trying to catch her attention could not mean good things for her. She rounded a bend and there it was, the gate in the wall. Footsteps sounded behind her and she picked up the pace.

'Hey!' The voice was louder now and she recognised it as belonging to Griffiths, the mutton-headed fool from earlier. 'I'm talking to you, girl. You'll stop if you know what's good for you.'

Ari growled. Being called a girl was only marginally less bad than being called a thing. She was a woman, and proud of it. But she didn't turn around to correct the buffoon. She was close to the gate and could leave the town in a matter of moments. She had no doubt that she could outrun Griffiths; the man looked like he would keel over if he took more than a few quick steps.

A flash of red up ahead had her coming to a complete stop. That small glimpse of fabric was the exact same colour as Sir Leopold's surcoat. But that would be impossible. There was no way he had made it to the gate before her. She'd had a head start; she'd clearly seen him looking down at her from the window. He could not have followed her through the tiny window and she was sure she had come the quickest route through the streets. They had been together all day and she would have noticed if he had been mapping out the streets, wouldn't she? But then, she had been busy doing exactly that herself and he hadn't had her full attention. He'd had the same amount of time to work out a route as well as the skill and the inclination. Damn him for making her question herself.

She ducked into a recessed doorway, her heart pounding. Perhaps she was imagining the bolt of red. She peered around the frame, and there was that flash of red again. It was exactly like the colour Sir Leopold wore.

She slipped from her hiding place. She would need to get closer to find out if it was really him. She glanced at the sky. The sun hadn't entirely set yet and—

'I'm glad you saw sense and stopped. I would have made life much harder for you if you had not heeded my words.' Ari groaned at Griffiths's approach. Why had she caught the attention of this bumbling fool in this moment? She had enough to contend with; she didn't need to add dealing with this witless oaf to her troubles.

'Go away, Griffiths.' She laced her command with all the contempt she felt.

'What did you say to me?' His outrage was palpable but Ari didn't spare him a glance, her attention focused on the gate and who may or may not be waiting for her there.

'I told you to go away. I don't have time for this.'

'Listen, little girl—' But he got no further before Ari was holding a blade to his throat.

'No, you listen, Griffiths. You are severely mistaken if you think this is going to end in any way other than with your humiliation and me walking away. Now, I will tell you one more time. Go away, leave me be and do not, for the love of all that is holy, ever call me a girl again. I have more important matters to settle than dealing with you and so I will let you go with only a warning this time.'

Griffiths's eyes bulged, his skin mottling with red splotches. 'How dare you! I am the lord's constable. You think a blade makes you—'

Ugh, she really did not have time for this. She shoved him, and he stumbled over his own feet several times before he landed on his backside, spluttering obscenities as he fell. She left him where he was. No doubt he would come after her but she had other problems to worry about at this moment.

She slipped down a short, narrow street, deciding to approach the gate from a different angle. She made it to the end without any footsteps pursuing her and as she slipped between a narrow gap in the buildings she had to hope that Griffiths had given up the chase or that he wouldn't think to look for her here.

She wiggled to the end of the gap and peered out towards the gate. From her new vantage point, she had a very good view of the gate and the surrounding area. Her heart sank as she saw who lounged against the inside archway. Sir Leopold flipped his new blade over and studied the tip before flipping it over once more. He was the very study of relaxation and calm, although she didn't doubt he was watching out for her intently.

Hmm, what to do? She wriggled back into her hiding place and began to plot.

How Arianwen thought she was going to get out of this one, Leo wasn't sure. He should just stride down to her hiding place, pull her out of it and carry her back to the inn, but part of him wanted to teach her that no matter how hard she tried, she would not escape him. Another part of him, the part that he was trying—and failing—to push away, found this whole situation appealing and was hard to keep leashed. The passionate, jump-in-with-both-feet side. He wanted to give her a chance to try to outwit him, and knew that it would give him a thrill that couldn't be replicated by a slow ride through the countryside. He could almost hear Hugh telling him what a bad idea this was but Hugh wasn't here right now and neither were his parents, and so he was going to follow his own instincts and hope that they didn't punch him in the face. So, he waited.

There was no other way out of the town, he was sure of that, but he had spoken to the guards at the gate to confirm. If Arianwen wanted to leave this evening, she would have to come this way. It was a shame she had spotted him waiting, but now she was going to try a different tack and he was keen to see what she came up with. When they were reunited, and after he'd made it very clear she would not be able to trick him by a simple kiss again, and after he'd railed at her for putting herself in danger, he'd demand she tell him what her plan really was about. He'd been mistaken before; this was not some young woman running from an undesirable marriage, although he was sure that was part of it. She was too organised, too disciplined, in her escape attempts. She did not come across as a young woman panicking about the prospect of marriage. This was something else and he was desperate to know what was going on in that mind of hers.

A cry from around the corner had him pushing himself upright. That had sounded like Arianwen. It came again. Yes, it was her. What was she up to now? He jogged slowly in the direction of the noise, hoping he wasn't making a colossal mistake in leaving the gate unguarded. He was sure she was trying to play him at his own game, but if he got it wrong and she was in real danger… No, that did not bear thinking about. This was partly a serious attempt to escape her marriage, but Leo also knew that it was a thrilling game to her, too. She wanted to beat him, to pit her wits against him and win. Nobody bested him at battle strategy, not even the most beautiful woman he had ever encountered.

He rounded the corner and his heart caught in his throat. Griffiths, the slimy toad from earlier, was towering over her, grinning as he held a blade close to her chest.

'Stop! Get away from her!' Leopold yelled out, ire coating the world red.

His distraction worked as Griffiths spun to react to this new threat. Arianwen didn't wait for a moment. As soon as Griffiths let go of her she began to run back into the town.

'Damn,' muttered Leo as Griffiths set off in pursuit,

realising as he did so that this was exactly what she wanted to happen. She wanted to lead both men on a chase through the streets because that took Leo away from the gate. It was clever and as his feet pounded along the cobbled streets, he couldn't stop the appreciative smile that spread across his face. She'd come up with a clever plan under pressure, one that had the potential to work because Leo couldn't afford to leave her to the mercies of her pursuer in order to guard the gate. If anything happened to her at the hands of Griffiths, Leo would be responsible.

Thankfully, Griffiths wasn't fast and Leo was able to get the man in his sights within a couple of streets. Arianwen was leading them on a merry dance through the winding lanes, away from the gate. Even as he sprinted after her, he couldn't help but admire her tactics. She was trying to disorient them and tire them out. She wasn't to know that he could keep this pace up all day and all night if he had to. It was what he was trained for. He was confident he could catch her if he kept his wits about him.

Arianwen, on the other hand, did not have long before she needed to make her final move. She would need to get to the gate before the sun set completely because the gate would be closed from that point onwards. If he wasn't so worried about what Griffiths would do to her, he would head straight to the gate and await her there, but Griffiths was an unknown quantity, and he would rather follow her to ensure her safety than achieve a tactical advantage.

He rounded a bend and came to a stop. Arianwen had a blade he had not seen before pressed to Griffiths's throat. 'I told you to leave me alone. Don't think I won't slit your throat and leave you on the ground to die.' Leo blinked; he had not expected such ferocity. Something hot and powerful surged through him, something so primal that it nearly brought him to his knees.

Arianwen looked up and caught his gaze and, for a moment, everything else ceased to exist. Then, for the second time that evening, she used his distraction to knock him off balance. She shoved Griffiths towards him and took off running once more. Leo staggered as Griffiths barrelled into him. He nearly went down under the weight of the oaf, but he just managed to keep his feet. Griffiths was spluttering with rage, trying but failing to shove his blade into Leo's face. Leo pushed Griffiths to one side, ignoring him as he shouted vile retribution on both him and Arianwen. Instead, Leo sprinted in the direction Arianwen had gone.

Arianwen was quick. He only caught glimpses of her skirts as they both dashed through the streets towards the gate, but he was quicker. He was gaining on her and, as the gate came into view once more, he was close enough to see her lips move in muttered curses. He couldn't help the grin that burst from him. This was the most excitement he'd had in a long time and he couldn't help but enjoy it.

Arianwen was so close to the gate now that she could almost touch it and part of him, the part that desperately admired her, wanted to see her succeed. The other part, the sensible, forward-thinking part, knew that this was not possible. Not only would it mean failure for both him and his brothers in arms, but he also couldn't let a young woman wander around at night alone. Arianwen might be far more skilled than he'd initially realised, but she was still in his charge and her safety was his responsibility until he handed her over to her betrothed.

Her foot was almost underneath the archway when he caught her in his arms.

'No…!' Her anguished cry cut through him. If this was a game to him, it was certainly not to her.

'I'm sorry,' he murmured into her hair, as she struggled in his arms. 'But I cannot let you go.' The portcullis began its creaking descent and Arianwen slumped against him. She was shaking in his arms, but he couldn't let her go to check whether that was from anger or from tears because there was still time for her to run from him. He would catch her again but then they might be locked outside the castle walls while their belongings and the safety of the inn were on the inside.

A guard came towards them. 'Is everything all right, sir?' he asked.

'No,' cried Arianwen. 'This man is taking me somewhere against my will.'

'Is that right, sir?'

Arianwen stiffened in Leo's arms, no doubt in reaction to her words being ignored in favour of him.

'Her father has entrusted her to my care and I act for him in this matter,' Leo said.

'He is not my father!' Arianwen roared, but Leo knew that he had won. Her outburst had worked against her and the guard was on his side. When he threw Arianwen over his shoulder and the guard didn't protest, he knew he was right.

As he strode away from the gate, he heard the portcullis clanging into place; there was no way out of the town now. Arianwen heard it, too, and stopped struggling, slumping dejectedly in his arms. He could let her down now, but he was strangely reluctant to do so.

'To think I felt sorry for you,' said his captive, her voice stiff with anger. 'Well, I won't from now on.'

'In what way did you feel sorry for me?' If anything, it was the other way around. He was desperately sorry for her. He wanted to let her go. Hell, he wanted to take her away but he could not.

'When I get away—and I will—you won't become one of the King's Knights. I felt bad about that before but now I don't.'

'I see.'

She muttered something under her breath, something about guilt and a kiss, and his grip on her tightened as something he hoped was fury shot through him. He was not going to think about that moment in the corridor, nor even talk to her about it. He should never have given in to the temptation to cover her mouth with his ,and he would not do so again. Even as he thought about it, an insidious voice in his head told him he was lying to himself. He pushed the thought aside; he had enough to deal with right now.

'You *will* tell me your plan and you will *not* escape from me again. Aside from anything else, it is too dangerous for you to be running about by yourself.'

She snorted. 'The only danger comes from you.'

'Me?' he snarled, truly angry for the first time. 'I am doing everything I can to protect you, to prevent you making a very dangerous mistake. You may think you are prepared to run about the countryside by yourself but that small blade is not going to be enough to protect you, no matter how skilled you might be.'

'I'm more skilled than you will ever know.'

'You're wrong. I will know everything about you by the time our evening has come to an end because you are going to tell it to me. Now.' He pushed his way into the inn, ignoring the patrons who stared at them as he strode through, Arianwen still over his shoulder. She bounced against his back as he climbed the stairs.

'Careful,' she growled.

'See. You're too precious to even make it up the stairs without complaining.'

'Fine. If you do not want to take care, don't say I didn't warn you.' Her elbows connected with his back with every step he took. It was like being jabbed with a blunt fork—annoying but ultimately nothing that would stop him.

Fortunately, he'd only broken the lock when he'd pushed into the room earlier, and the rest of the chamber door was still intact. He strode over to the bed and unceremoniously dumped her onto it. She immediately tried to scramble off but he caught her arm. Before she could move any farther, he removed his belt and tied her arm to the bedpost.

'Hey!' she cried, tugging on her binding and causing his body to tighten in a way that had nothing to do with his fury for her. He took a step back. 'What do you think you are doing?' she demanded, her lips curled in a snarl.

'What I should have done earlier—making it impossible for you to get away from me.'

Her eyes burned with rage. She tugged on his belt but he had tied it tightly, and she would not be able to get away.

He strode over to the window and pulled the shutters

closed, grateful when the chamber darkened. He adjusted himself beneath his clothing. His body shouldn't be hardening because of the wildcat on the bed but, damn him, it was. He wanted to push her onto her back and keep her there while they both slaked their fury in the most animalistic of ways. But this time, he was not going to let his impulses take over. He was going to be calm and considered, and be more like Hugh than he had ever managed before.

For a long moment, he kept his back to her, listening to her muttering curses, which called into doubt his legitimacy, curses he'd never heard from a woman before. He willed his body to calm down. He needed to be rational, needed to make it clear that she would not get away from him again, but for reasons he could not understand, her anger was only making him harder.

He picked up the only chair in the chamber and carried it over so that he was level with her. He sank down into it gratefully, arranging his clothes so that she would have no idea of the effect she was having on him.

'Now,' he said, his voice not betraying his inner turmoil, 'you will tell me everything.'

Ari stared at the warrior sitting opposite her. If he came close to her, then he would see just how powerful she could be. She would fight tooth and nail, grab his hair and pull his mouth to hers and kiss him until he could no longer breathe. No, wait. Kiss him! Where had that thought come from? Just because they had shared a tantalisingly brief moment earlier did not mean she wanted to repeat it, especially with the man who had destroyed her plans. There would be no more kissing.

Time was running out, they were getting closer to Lord Cradoc's castle and her terror of being trapped into a marriage she could never escape was filling her with a fury that burned brighter than any fire she had ever witnessed. Anger was better than despair, for despair would drag her down while her ire would keep her motivated. The opportunities for her to get away were going to be fewer, and the chances of getting caught even higher. She had underestimated her opponent, had allowed herself to like him, even to crave the touch of him, and in doing so she had failed, yet again, to plan sufficiently to get away from him.

'Talk,' he growled.

His anger sent a jolt of something liquid through her veins, a hot, fiery sensation that was nothing to do with the rage coursing through her. There was something else going on here. This was not just about her escape; there was something between them, something that had her skin tingling and caused the urge to touch any part of him in order to get some respite from the strange, squirming frustration. She turned away from him. Maybe if she couldn't see him she could regain some composure.

'Look at me.'

She shook her head.

'I want to see it in your eyes when you lie to me.'

That had her turning back to face him. 'I have never lied about my intentions to get away from you,' she growled. 'You know I don't want to marry Lord Cradoc. If you were a true knight, you would let me go.' As soon as she'd said the words, she wished she could cram them back into her mouth. She could see she had hurt him more than any physical blow could. The ensuing silence was painful to the point of ruination. 'I didn't mean that,' she said when she could no longer take his silent recrimination.

'I know,' he said softly, some of the anger seeping out of his expression. 'I can see it by the look on your face. I also know that this is painful for you and I wish there was something I could do to make it better, but I also know that I can't.'

Some of her fury melted away in the compassion she could hear in his voice. 'I will never stop trying to escape,' she said quietly.

'And I will never let you get away,' he answered equally as quietly and equally as firmly.

'Then we are at an impasse.'

He let out a long breath and rested his elbows on his knees, leaning closer to her. 'An impasse would suggest that there is no way out for either of us.'

She closed her eyes, breaking the hold he seemed to have over her. She may be beaten in this round but she would not give up fighting for her freedom until the very end.

'We should rest,' he said, the chair scraping against the wooden floor as he stood. 'We have another long day tomorrow.' She heard his footsteps move closer, then the touch of his fingers on her wrist as he untied his belt. 'Move over,' he said gruffly when her arm was free from the binding.

Her eyes flew open. 'We are not going to share a bed.'

'Yes, we are.'

'But—'

'Lady Arianwen, you have tried to escape from me twice. I would be a fool to sleep anywhere other than right next to you. You may think yourself lucky that I do not tie myself to you. I'm not leaving your side again for the rest of the trip.'

Ice dripped through her veins. 'What if I need to go to the privy?'

'I will come with you.'

'What if you need to go to the privy?'

'You will come with me.' She wrinkled her nose but didn't protest. Hopefully, one journey to do that would rid her of this inconvenient attraction to him. She could not afford to fail next time. He may be good—far better than she had anticipated—but she was desperate and that gave her an edge.

'I know what you're thinking.'

'You do?'

'Mmm… You're thinking I will never see you on the privy because you're going to outsmart me tomorrow.' That was so shockingly accurate she didn't know how to respond. 'Am I right?'

'No.' Her answer sounded hesitant even to her own ears so she didn't blame him when he laughed.

'You're not going to, by the way. Outsmart me, that is. Now, move over so we can both get some rest.' The bed dipped as he climbed onto the mattress next to her. She rolled over so she was facing away from him. He cleared his throat. 'You have nothing to fear from me. I will not take advantage of you. You will arrive at your wedding a maiden still.'

'I'm not concerned about that.' She wasn't. He didn't need a mattress at an inn to take her against her will. If he'd been that way inclined, he could have done so the very first night they had been on the road. She hadn't missed the way he looked at her because it was the same way she looked at him: with longing and with an irritation that the longing existed in the first place.

As she lay here next to Leopold, the scent of leather and woodland filling the air, she felt the smallest inkling of what might have possessed her father to give up his life in Windsor for her mother. He had wanted to be with his wife more than he had wanted to make a name for himself. Although Ari would never make that decision herself, she was beginning to understand what might drive a person to it. She *wanted* to roll over to face Leopold, to finally know what his short beard felt like beneath her fingertips, beneath her lips. She *wanted* to know what it was like to be held in his arms when he was not carrying her over his shoulder, and she wanted him to *want* her with the same intensity. Leopold with his restrained temper, his otherwise easy-going manner, his skills and his luxuriously wide shoulders was the first man to ever tempt her in this way, and this made him dangerous. If he knew how she was beginning to feel, he might be able to get her to give up on her dreams not by telling her to do so but by asking.

'Are you going someplace where you can use your fighting skills?' Sir Leopold asked.

She twitched. How like him to guess the heart of the matter. 'Where would I go to do that? No one is going to accept a woman.'

There was a beat of silence and then he said, 'Which is why you cut your hair, isn't it? To make you look like a boy.'

She didn't answer. How was he figuring all this out?

'It's all making sense now. The way you moved today,

your ability to strategise under pressure, your handling of your dagger…it's all so much better than many of the trained men I know.' Despite the unravelling of her secrets, she couldn't help the swell of pride that bloomed within her. A compliment from him about her fighting abilities meant a lot to her—far more than it should.

'Good night, Sir Leopold,' she said, not answering his question.

'Shall we dispense with the *sir*? I feel as if we have gone past that. My friends call me Leo.'

'My friends call me Ari.'

'Good night, Ari.'

'I didn't say you were one of them,' she countered quickly.

He laughed softly.

'Good night, Leo.'

Chapter Eleven

Ari must have been tired because she fell asleep almost as soon as they stopped talking, but Leo lay staring up into the darkness long after the tavern had settled down for the night.

Tonight had been…frustrating, infuriating and undeniably exhilarating. The chase, trying to outwit Ari and adding in a real foe, his anger, her defiance…it was everything that got his blood pumping. The unpredictability of it all called to the warrior in him.

But that wasn't what was keeping him awake. Ari was safe with him. He would not touch her but that didn't stop his imagination. She murmured in her sleep, turning so that her face was close to his. Her normally animated features were still, her lips soft. Earlier today had been the first time he'd kissed a woman. He'd moved instinctively and if Ari hadn't shoved him, he would have carried on. Hell, he had no idea whether he would have stopped himself or whether his impulsive nature would have broken free and taken them to the point of no return. It was good that she had ended it—excellent, really, and so the pain in his chest as he remembered it made no sense.

He propped himself up on his elbow and gazed down at her. She was facing away from him, her short hair spilling out towards him. His fingers itched to thread themselves through it, to allow the silky strands to slide over and around them, to trace the length of her spine and make her arch towards him with the same want he had for her. But touching her without her knowledge would be creepy and so he only gazed down at her until his senses returned.

'Pathetic,' he muttered, throwing himself backwards so that he was lying facing the ceiling once more.

Ugh, if his friends could see him now they would laugh heartily. He'd never been one to moon after a woman, not when there were new skills to learn and sword fighting techniques to perfect. And now, this woman, who wanted nothing to do with him, who was desperate to get away from him, was bringing him to his knees and she didn't even realise it. Would she care if she knew? He had no doubt she would be kind, would perhaps let him down in a gentle, teasing manner but no, he doubted very much his regard for her was returned. The look of disgust on her face when they'd talked about love told him everything he needed to know. She was not thinking the same as him. Although there had been that hungry look in her eyes when he'd tied her to the bed earlier, he had so little experience that he could not tell if it had been desire or hatred.

He drew a hand down his face. This thinking was entirely irrelevant anyway. She was betrothed to another man and, even if she adored Leo and was willing to give up whatever dream she had that kept her running away from him, that fact wouldn't change. Nor would it change the reasons why he was on this mission in the first place. Perhaps if it was just *his* life plan hanging in the balance, if he didn't have to worry about letting Hugh and Tristan down or disappointing his parents, then he would confess to her how he was beginning to feel. No, there was no *perhaps* about it. If it was just him, he would not take her to Lord Cradoc's castle, would do everything he could to keep her away from the man and the stepfather who had made her feel unloved. Then he would spend the rest of his life trying to prove that he was worthy of her, following her to the ends of the earth if he had to. But he was not the only person in this mess, and he would never let Tristan and Hugh down just to follow his own desires. Nor could he imagine the horror of his parents when he brought shame to their family and ran off with another man's bride.

It worried him to the very pit of his stomach that he could even contemplate giving up on the dreams he had wanted for so long.

'Which is why,' he said to the air above him, 'you must be constant in your convictions. If you can be turned by a pretty face one week, then who knows what will distract you next.' Not that Ari was only a pretty face—she was brave and funny and smart and—

He was doing it again. He rolled over onto his stomach and buried his face in the mattress. Maybe if he couldn't see or smell her, he would finally get some respite from this endless cycle of thoughts.

He woke some time later to the flutter of fingers against his jaw. He blinked groggily as the chamber came into focus. Next to him, Ari muttered something about horses, her breath whispering over his forehead.

While they'd both slept, he'd turned onto his side facing her and she'd rolled towards him and now her body was flush with his, her hand resting lightly below his jaw.

'Bel,' she muttered, and tapped his jaw once more.

He grinned. She thought he was her horse. He was looking forward to her waking so that he could tease her. He couldn't wait to see the look on her face, the one that she had when she pretended to be irritated with him but was secretly amused.

The next moment, his smile dropped completely as her fingers traced down the length of his neck, the sensation exquisitely intense. He stayed still, loath to wake her from her dream to put an end to her delicate touch.

'Warm,' she said, moving closer until her head was resting against his chest. He was surprised the pounding of his heart did not wake her. His body was in turmoil. Every part of him yearned to pull her closer still, to bury his nose in her hair and inhale her. He wanted to trace the curve of her neck, wanted to press his hand to her back, to map her skin with his mouth and yet he knew that he could not, that to do so would cross a boundary that could destroy them both. Her hand was moving now, tracing the length of his arm, and he shivered as tremors followed in the wake of her palm. He needed to stop this before his senses took over his mind and he forgot himself.

'Arianwen,' he whispered, his voice hoarse.

'Mmm.'

'Arianwen, it's time to wake up.'

She shook her head, the movement sending a spear of lust shooting through him. He groaned and she mumbled something incoherent.

'Ari, wake up, I beg of you.' His voice was hoarse. 'We have a long way to go today.' He needed to remind himself of the practicalities, the reason they were both here in this chamber. She was not his woman, even as his body screamed out that he wanted to make her his.

Some of the softness left her form and she stretched her legs, the movement causing her to rub up against him. There was nothing he could do to hide his body's reaction to her being so close, and he knew she'd felt his hardness when she froze. Slowly, so slowly she was barely moving, she tilted her face until she was looking up at him. Their gazes met and held.

She didn't move away, and neither did he.

The urge to move against her, to provide some release to the ache that was building up inside him, was phenomenal but he held himself still. For all Arianwen's courage, she was still a maiden, and he would not grope her. But it was all he could do to hold himself still; he could not have moved away from her if the King of England himself demanded it. His reason was deserting him quicker than a man drunk on ale.

Her hand on his arm began moving again, feather-light against his sleeve. He grunted when her fingertip reached his palm. She moved down the length of it, sending more of those delicious tingles coursing through his body. Her fingers slipped into his and they threaded their hands together.

'What is this?' she murmured.

He had no idea what she meant; all his rational thought had gone. 'What is what?' he managed to mumble.

'This feeling. It's coming to me all the time now.' She moved against him and he groaned, a deep, guttural sound that filled the room. She moved again and his head fell back, his eyes closed. The movement had produced no relief from the desperate ache inside him, only intensifying the sensation.

'I know I should move away from you,' she continued.

'Yes.'

No, no, anything but that.

'But I don't want to.'

'No.'

'Do you want me to?'

'No.' She moved against him and he couldn't help it. He pushed back, relishing her desperate gasp. He was not alone in this moment. Sensation was building within him, quickly and more intensely than he had ever experienced before. If he was not careful, he would spend himself in his clothes in an embarrassingly short time.

'Are you in pain?' she asked.

'No. It's…' How to explain this sensation within him when he wasn't sure himself? His previous experience had not taught him anything about this.

He could feel her smile against the curve of his arm. 'Are you able to answer with more than one word?'

It was amazing he could think at all. 'No.'

She laughed quietly. His hand gripped the blanket in a tight fist as the movement nearly sent him spiralling over the edge.

His knee fell forward, sliding between her legs, and she gasped as she settled on his thigh, her fingers tightening in his grip.

'Oh!' She sounded as breathless as he felt. 'I want…' She moved against him, rocking against his leg, and he saw stars.

He held her still.

'This is a bad idea.'

If they went further, if he took her innocence, then he would have to marry her and the consequences would be so far reaching as to bring down his world. A small part of him whispered, *I could create a new world. A better world.* Thinking of his future while in the grip of whatever this was, was not a good idea.

'We're not doing anything.'

She moved…or he moved…something happened and he wasn't holding her still anymore. Where was his will-power? The strength he prided himself on? It was lying on its side, begging her to touch him, to do anything that would end this tortuous need, and if that made him pathetic then he no longer cared. His body reminded him that this was the first time he had ever held a woman in his arms and enjoyed it; he might never experience this again. Her fingers were on his neck, in his hair, she was pulling, stroking, sending him wild. He had to do something, anything, that would bring him release… but he must stop short of the act that would ruin her for her marriage bed.

Unable to take it anymore, he rolled onto his back, bringing her with him, settling her core against his length. He could not feel her, not through all their clothes, but the weight of her lying on him was enough. By the look in her eyes this new position was good for her, too. The sensation of her lying there was like nothing he'd experienced before. He wanted… Hell, he wasn't even sure what it was that he wanted. For this to never end, for it to stop, for the ache to spiral into something else, something more.

He slipped one hand into the hair he'd longed to touch. 'This had better not be a ruse to distract me.'

Even as he said the words he realised he was so far gone that he didn't care if it was, so long as he got the release he so desperately needed.

'It's… I…'

He shifted and her eyes rolled back in her head. She was as gone as he was and his blood roared with triumph.

His hands slipped to the curve at the base of her spine and he pressed her gently but firmly towards him.

'Oh…'

Her mouth fell open. She lifted herself up slightly so she could look at him directly. 'Is that…?' She wriggled and he grunted. She moved again and he gripped her hips to stop her.

'Yes, that is what you think it is and you need to stop moving. I can't think when you do that.'

She tried to move again but he held firm, even as his body yelled at him to let her do whatever she liked.

'This, what you're feeling, what I am feeling, too, is desire. I can stop.' She shook her head, her lips were parted and her eyes were glazed. 'We won't… I won't… You will still be a maid… I won't even touch…but I can make this ache between us better and… Do you want me to?'

'Yes,' she breathed.

'Are you sure? Because—'

'Sometimes you talk too much.' Her voice was breathless but there was that teasing light in her eyes, the look he was beginning to adore.

'You'll never know how grateful I am that you don't want to stop. I'm going to…'

His hands settled on the round globes of her buttocks,

his mind completely taken over by what they were doing right here, right now.

'Oh, yes,' she murmured, placing her hands on the mattress on either side of his chest. She was holding herself slightly above him, her gaze raking over his face, his neck, his chest. He squeezed his fingers and she moaned. Damn, she was delicious, the perfect size for him. He'd love to sink his fingers into her flesh here, to caress her curves and to take his time learning every dip and hollow. *Later*, his mind told him. Later, he would take his time but now...

He dragged her up his length and back down, once... twice...again.

'That feels... I've never...' She panted, her gaze rolling backwards, and he growled in satisfaction, exultant that she was experiencing the same pleasure he was. 'I... Oh... Leo...' She cried out, rocking against him now under her own momentum. Her arms gave out and her head dropped to the crook of his neck, her breath brushing across his skin. 'I never knew...'

'Me neither.' His very limited experience had not prepared him for this. Nothing had prepared him for the way his body sang to hers.

They rocked together, her moans and gasps of pleasure urging him on. Nothing had ever felt this good. Finally, he understood what other men raved about. This. This was everything and also not enough. It was a primal heat that was building at the core of him. He pressed her closer still, moving her faster and harder and she was muttering incoherently into his neck. And then they were crying out together and he was spilling into his clothes in an endless wave of ecstasy.

She slumped down onto him and he wrapped his arms around her, holding her tightly, pressing her to him as if he could make them one.

'Your heart is going very fast,' she murmured. 'Or is it mine? I can't tell.'

Leo could only grunt, his words deserting him completely.

'Perhaps it's both.'

'Perhaps,' he managed to whisper.

As his heart rate returned to normal, he became aware of the dampness on his stomach. He should move and clean himself up, but he was so very, very tired. His eyelids fluttered shut and he slept.

Ari lay within the cage of Leo's arms. After whatever had happened to them had finished, his breathing had turned soft and heavy and she was sure the big man was deeply asleep. From the light coming in around the edge of the shutters, she could tell that it was some time past dawn. The gates would be open once more and she could make her escape. For a reason she couldn't fathom, she was reluctant to move. No, that was a lie. She knew exactly why she was not going to make her escape, and it was all because of the man lying beneath her.

She wasn't tired. She had slept surprisingly well given the circumstances, and she hadn't changed her mind about leaving Leo at the first opportunity but... It didn't seem honourable to sneak away with her body still humming with joy at what he'd done to her. She didn't want to think about the thought buzzing at the back of her consciousness that it would be hard to leave him not because he would track her down, but because being apart from him would cause her pain. She would need to think on this, but it was impossible with his strong arms around her. So, fool that she was, she laid her head against his chest and breathed him in.

She had some idea of what had passed between them. She was a maid but not a total innocent. She'd known exactly what she could feel beneath her when he'd pulled her on top of him. She understood the basics of how a baby was made and knew that men and sometimes women, enjoyed the experience, but she'd had no idea that her body could feel that way, that total abandonment of good sense and reason would flood her as she had chased an ending she had never known existed. Leo had given her a gift and she would always be grateful to him, even after she had left him.

Maybe it was the regular thump of his heart, or the way her body fitted perfectly against his, or maybe she hadn't slept as well as she'd thought because in moments, she had drifted off also.

She awoke as Leo tried to slip from underneath her.

'Sorry,' he muttered. 'I didn't mean to wake you. I just need to…' He gestured to his stomach and she frowned. She had no idea what he was talking about and he did not elaborate.

Instead, he made his way over to the bowl of water and stripped to his skin, his moves precise and contained. She pushed herself up slightly and looked her fill, reasoning that he would not have undressed if he minded her looking. He was as muscled as she'd imagined, although she had not seen his legs or buttocks before. She could not see the part of him that had been long and hard beneath her but the sight before her was still spectacular.

He cleaned himself quickly but he didn't pull his undergarments back on. Instead, he put on his shirt and pulled his surcoat over it. He crammed the clothes he was no longer wearing into one of his bags, all the while not looking at her. When he was done, he straightened and turned towards her, his gaze landing somewhere above her head, his whole posture rigid. While she had been busy gazing at him, he had obviously been having a very different conversation with himself.

'I must apologise for what happened between us. I took advantage of you and it was wrong. No, *I* was wrong. I knew what I was doing and you did not, and I should never have done such a thing. I know it cannot happen again.' Even his tone of voice sounded different, more formal and certainly tenser.

'Why not?'

She knew why not. They both had places they wanted to be, things they needed to achieve, and yet she wanted him to forget and for him to make her forget, for this chamber to become their everything, if only for a while.

He swallowed. 'It is wrong because you are betrothed to another man.'

She shrugged, affecting a nonchalance she did not feel. She had never thought of herself as promised to the man who had not once spoken to her during their brief meeting. She had never made an oath that she would marry him. The whole arrangement had been made by her stepfather, who wanted her out of his hair so that he could finally be free of his wife's child with her late husband.

'I have never had, nor ever will have, any intention of marrying Lord Cradoc.'

He smiled sadly, finally meeting her gaze. She could see the depths of his sorrow there and she knew that he meant what he was saying, but that didn't stop the words cutting like a blade.

'It makes no difference. As far as I am concerned, you are going to marry him and what I did earlier was wrong. You are an innocent and I took advantage of you. Nothing like that will happen between us again.'

How dare he! He might think he was going to deliver her to Lord Cradoc but she was the one in control, not her stepfather and not Leo. She rolled over and climbed out of the bed.

'Fine.'

It wasn't fine. It was so far away from fine that she didn't know how she was going to keep her true feelings hidden inside, but she would. He would never know how much his rejection stung.

'Fine?' He raised an eyebrow.

'Yes, fine,' she repeated. 'As we will soon be parting ways, it matters not.'

She walked past him and splashed some water onto her face. Her skin was burning as if she had a chill and yet she knew she did not. She knew the feverish burning had only started after his cool dismissal. The cold water did nothing to calm her but it gave her a few moments in which she wasn't looking at Leo. She patted her face dry until she was sure her expression didn't reveal how much he had hurt her. She was being ridiculous. He was her captor, and as attractive as she might find him, as much as she was coming to enjoy his company, as much as he might be the only man she had ever felt anything for, they were at odds and would never be anything but opponents in this battle of wills.

She had taken nothing out of the bag that was supposed to be accompanying her to Lord Cradoc's castle and her own bag that contained her rations, so she did not need to adjust either of them. She was packed and ready to go. She picked up the small bag containing all her belongings, leaving the other one for Leo to deal with, and slung it over her shoulder.

'You're in my way,' she said to him when he remained as still as a statue. 'You need to move.'

She wanted to press her hands to his chest and shove him out of the way but she only gripped the strap of her bag tighter.

'You seem angry,' he said.

'I'm not.' She was. The strap dug into the palm of her hand as she clutched it tightly. In the back of her mind, she knew what he had said was rational, but somehow his rejection was the worst in a long string of similar refusals, all allegedly for her own good. She was a woman, so she couldn't fight. She was now a lord's stepdaughter so she could not befriend the castle servants any more. She was no longer a girl and so she needed to marry. None of this was what she wanted and yet these were all decisions made for her.

He tilted his head to one side. 'You're like a wet cat, all spikey and cross.'

'A wet cat?' she growled, holding her head high. 'I am not a cat nor any other animal. I am Arianwen de Monfort.' She had not said her father's surname for many years, and it felt good to say it now.

'I'm sorry if I have upset or offended you today. I was not thinking earlier and now—'

'Argh!' she half screamed because it was better than crying. 'I am not upset, offended or cross. I am merely keen to get underway.'

'So that you may attempt to get away from me again.' His infuriating eyebrow rose. Fine, so that sight normally caused her stomach to flutter oddly, but right now it was condescending and she wanted to lean over and push it back in line with the other one.

She nodded. 'Exactly.'

'Right. So, to be completely clear and to make sure that you are not angry with me about my statement, what happened between us earlier won't happen again.' He was frowning now, as if he could not understand her at all, which he apparently couldn't. Any relationship she'd thought they were developing was clearly one-sided.

'I am as calm as I ever am,' she lied. 'And what happened between us earlier won't happen again, even if you beg.'

His lips curved into that half smile she normally liked so much but right now made her want to pull his hair out. 'I never beg for anything.'

'Good. Then this whole thing will not be an issue between us because I do not beg, either.'

'Good.'

They glared at each other for a long moment, Arianwen unsure whether this was part of their argument or something else. She only knew that she was relieved when he finally tore his gaze away.

'Let's go, then.'

'Finally,' she muttered as he moved to let her past.

As the door closed behind them, she was sure she heard him mutter, 'God help me, she's going to kill me.' But she couldn't be sure and she was not going to ask.

Chapter Twelve

Leo brought the horses to a standstill not long after midday. Arianwen was still a seething mass of anger and he couldn't say he blamed her. This morning he had taken advantage of her and, although she claimed to be fine that it wouldn't happen again, she very clearly was not. This was where his lack of experience was letting him down. He could not tell if she was angry at him for what they had done together or furious because he had said they could not do it again. The only thing he could be sure about was that she was very, very displeased with him, and he knew it had nothing to do with his not letting her escape from him. It was odd because *that* really should be the biggest cause of tension between them but it wasn't. It was as if they had lain out their battle lines on the issue and they both knew where they stood. But in this desire that swirled around them, they were equally as baffled as to what to do about it.

He should never have given in to the temptation this morning. He could argue that he hadn't been in his right mind when he had grabbed at her—he'd been no better than a dog after a bitch in heat—and while it was true he had not been thinking clearly, his actions spoke badly of him as a knight. An exemplary knight should always be in control of his actions, no matter the situation or the temptation. This morning Leo had been so far from controlled it was as if he had never even heard of the word.

So yes, he understood her anger; he was angry at himself. Not only had he taken advantage of her, he also had absolutely no intention of letting her get away from him. He would deliver her to her betrothed because that was what he had sworn to do and that was what was right. It may not be what he wanted—hell, it was so far from what he wanted that it would break his heart to part with her, but that was not the point. The point was that he was a knight. He followed a certain code of behaviour and that did not involve rutting against an innocent woman. He shuddered, but whether from shame or from latent desire he could not say, and he dared not dwell on it.

'We'll rest here,' he said to her back.

She shrugged. 'Very well.'

It had only been half a day, but he already missed the light, teasing banter between them. They both saw to their horses in a silence that was almost deadly for everything that was going unsaid. They settled beneath the sweeping shade of a large oak tree. He handed her some of the honeyed bread he'd bought especially for her. For a moment, it appeared as if she would say something. He held his breath but she merely muttered her appreciation and took it from him. While she ate, she watched the horses graze and he watched her.

He couldn't put his finger on what exactly drew him to her. She was beautiful, yes, although he didn't think hers was a traditional beauty. She had him bewitched, that was for sure. He rubbed his eyes. It was no use trying to identify her most attractive feature. Staring at her was only making him feel worse.

He made his way over to Bosco and pulled his sword from its scabbard. If they were going to exist in tortuous silence, it would be better if he made use of the time. He might as well use this time to go over some of the drills he normally performed daily but had recently neglected because of this mission. It would help him keep supple when there was a danger of him becoming too stiff after days on his horse. He began to move, losing himself in the repetitive rhythm. After a while, he moved on and then on again, the rhythm comforting until he reached the final one. This drill was one he had practised many times but one he still found hard. He was three steps into it when Arianwen spoke.

'You're doing it wrong.'

He froze, his sword arm extended awkwardly. 'No, I'm not.' He was and he knew it but if those were the first words she'd spoken to him since this morning, he would be damned if he was polite in return. He carried on as if they had not exchanged words.

'I am willing to believe that your back aches ferociously at the end of this exercise.'

'It never has.' It did, every single time. He carried on. She was desperate for him to ask for her advice but he would not.

'You're very close to getting it right.'

'I *am* getting it right.' His back twinged and he bit back a groan.

'That hurt, didn't it?'

'No.' *Yes.*

'Why are you being so stubborn?'

'I'm not being stubborn. I'm being truthful.'

He heard her bite into her apple, the sharp crunch irritating him more than he could explain.

'I could show you how to do it, if you like.'

He stopped and turned to her. 'You want me to hand over my sword?'

She shrugged nonchalantly. 'It would certainly help prevent your future bad back.'

'I won't have a bad back and I am not handing you my sword. I believe we went over this once before and that was before I knew of your nefarious plan.'

'You're afraid I will get the better of you.'

He snorted. 'You haven't yet.'

That bothered her; he could see it in the set of her shoulders. Good. She was annoying him, so now they were both irked. 'Maybe not yet, but I will.'

'Hmm.' He restarted his steps but during the conversation, he'd forgotten where he was. He was going to have to start again but if he did the exercises wrong twice, he was going to be in endless agony.

She huffed, pushing herself to her feet. 'Resume the second step.' He hesitated. 'Go on,' she said impatiently.

He put himself into position. It was not one he liked; he could not see the point of it. He was excellent with the sword and had proved himself so many times that nobody, not even Lord Ormand, doubted his ability. And yet, whenever he'd complained to his drill master about this routine, the man had said the same thing every time: 'This exercise will help with flexibility. You might not like it, but your body will thank you for it when you make it part of your daily practise.'

She stepped behind him and he forced himself to

stay still. She might be angry with him but she was not a killer. She would not stab him in the back, no matter how furious. She'd attack him from the front.

'You are not leaning backwards enough.' Her hands went to the base of his spine and she pushed. He let out a groan as she moved him. 'See, you're already hurting.' He said nothing. His groan was nothing to do with the position he was now holding with ease and everything to do with her touch. He had spent all morning berating himself for his actions in the bed, and one touch had him forgetting everything he had promised himself. If she gave the slightest indication that she would welcome him, he would throw his sword to the ground and forget every good intention he had ever had.

Touching him had been a mistake. It was much easier to remain angry with him when she was keeping her distance. Not that she was angry... She was determined and focused and...

Fine, she was angry, too. Extremely, blisteringly furious. She wasn't sure whether she wanted to whack him over the head with his own sword and dump him in a bush, or drag him into said bush and press her body to his once more. It was this extreme reaction to him that was pushing her to the edge of rationality this morning.

'Try the next move.' She was pleased that her voice retained its practical edge.

His movements were graceful and she'd enjoyed watching him perform the drills that she had practised in the privacy of her own chamber so that no one could see her. Her enjoyment was more than it should be but as soon as he'd started this one, he'd become stiff.

'What is it about this drill you don't enjoy?'

'It seems pointless,' he grumbled. 'I'm unlikely to attack an opponent while in this uncomfortable position.' He brandished his sword above his head.

She laughed. He turned to her, his eyes alight with triumph.

'I'm laughing at you, not with you.'

His eyes filled with mischief and her heart betrayed her by leaping at the sight. She pushed him into another position and his smile died.

'That was mean.'

'Now I am laughing.' She wasn't. Her hands were on his back, the muscles beneath his surcoat easy to feel. She wanted to sink her fingers into them and that was damned frustrating because he'd made it clear he didn't want to do that with her again. 'The point of this drill is flexibility. To be a better soldier, you must be able to bend and twist with ease.'

He straightened. 'Very well. You can show me how you would perform these movements.'

For a moment, she thought he was going to hand her his sword but he bent and passed her a fallen branch. She smirked at him; he rolled his eyes in return. She took the branch and weighed it in her hand. It was heavier than a sword but not too much. She swung it around experimentally. Leo leaned against a tree, watching her intently. She moved through the set of moves easily and then a second time more quickly, and this time her body thrilled at the chance to move unencumbered, to finally wield a weapon, even if it wasn't a real one.

'Impressive,' he said when she finally came to a stop.

She glanced across at him. Gone was the teasing light

in his eye, to be replaced by something else, something fierce and intense. Her chest tightened and she turned away from him.

'Would you like to spar with me?' he asked.

She stilled, her branch still held aloft. He wanted her to pit her skills against his. Nobody had wanted to fight with her for so long, not since her father had died. Her heart swelled until it felt as if it were pushing against her ribs.

For the briefest of moments, she considered not doing it. If she engaged with Leo, he would know her true skill level but the temptation overwhelmed her common sense. She had not sparred with anyone for so long and she knew her skill had suffered as a result. This was too good an opportunity to miss.

'I should like to spar with you. I hope you don't sulk when you lose.'

He grinned. 'Fighting talk. I like it.' He sheathed his sword and selected a branch of his own.

'Shall we make this interesting?' she asked as they circled each other.

'I'm going to regret asking this but go on.'

'If I win, you wish me luck and let me go.'

He laughed. 'I like your optimism but I will never agree to that.'

Their wooden swords met, the jolt reverberating up her arm. 'Are you that confident I will win?'

'No.' He shook his head vehemently. 'All right, how about this? I win and you come the rest of the way with me without an argument and without trying to escape. I hand you over to your betrothed and you wish me luck.'

She scowled. 'I would never agree to that.'

'Because you are that confident *I* will win.' He raised an eyebrow.

They exchanged a few more blows, then he lunged forward and she dodged easily.

'I win and you give me a head start next time I escape.'

'Again, no. I win and you tell me where you want to go so badly.'

She saw an advantage and pressed. In a move so quick she didn't see it, he stepped towards her, nearly knocking her off balance. 'An excellent parry,' she said as she regained her foothold.

'Your recovery wasn't bad.'

'My recovery was exemplary. I might also agree to your terms.'

'My terms?' They were both starting to pant now; sweat was beginning to bead on her forehead and she wiped it away with the back of her hand.

'Yes. I might tell you where I want to go so badly if you win.' Would it really matter if he knew? She wouldn't give him the exact details, there would be no mention of Denmark and King Edward, but she could give him the general idea. But only if she lost, which she wouldn't.

'And if you win?'

'You will at least consider letting me go without stopping me.'

He moved around the space, his eyes bleak. 'I cannot.'

Her heart hurt. 'You can't even consider it?'

'If it were just me, I might. Hell, I would do more than that. You shouldn't have to marry Lord Cradoc if you don't want to. I know that. If it was just me, I would help you fight against your stepfather's arrangement. But it isn't. If I fail to deliver you, I ruin the lives of Hugh and Tristan, too. They are more than brothers to me, Arianwen. They have been my family for years.'

'I do understand, Leo.' She really did, although it didn't make it any easier for her to accept. 'All I want from you is your word that you will consider it.'

'Very well. If you win, I will think about the idea of letting you run off, but Ari, I am more than sure that my answer will be the same.'

It wasn't much of a victory but it was better than she had hoped for. She began to fight in earnest, as if this really was a battle for her freedom. He responded to her volley with pressure of his own and for a long while all that could be heard was the loud thud of wood on wood as they battled for dominance.

Her muscles began to ache but she would rather die than admit it. She no longer wiped the sweat away and it dripped past her eye.

'Are you ready to yield?' he asked.

'Never.'

He laughed. 'I do not know anyone as stubborn as you. I really believe you would fight until the end of all time rather than concede.'

'The reason you think that is because you are the same. Are *you* ready to concede?'

He was still smiling as he thrust at her. 'I don't need to concede because I am winning.'

'You're arrogant and pig-headed and...'

He knocked the branch out of her hand and it sailed in a high arc before hitting the bark of a tree with a resounding crack.

'And I'm today's victor.'

He dropped his own branch. Sweat coated his face and he was breathing heavily. The same strange desire she'd had earlier came over her. She wanted to push him to the ground and wipe that infuriating smile off his face. Annoyingly, the only way she could picture it was by pressing her own mouth to his, and that wasn't going to happen. His smile slowly faded as they gazed at each other. An odd silence was building and that strange pull was back, the one that made it nearly impossible to turn away from him. She should joke and tease or poke at him like she normally did, but she couldn't find the words. He was the first to look away, seemingly studying the ground by his feet.

'You fight well,' he said, still looking down.

'Not well enough, it would seem.'

'You nearly got the best of me many times.' He wiped his forehead with his sleeve. 'That rarely happens. No.' He shook his head. 'I must give you your due, even though it pains me. That never happens. I have not had a bout last that long in…' He shrugged. 'I don't think I've ever had a sparring session last for more than a few moments. You have real talent.'

Warmth unfurled inside her, spreading from her chest to the very tips of her toes. It had been an eternity since anyone had complimented her skills.

'If you hand me over to Lord Cradoc, I will never be able to fight again.'

His shoulders sagged. 'I am sorry, Arianwen, more than you will ever know. But Tristan and Hugh are—'

'I know. They're your family and you don't want to let them down.' She couldn't argue with that. Her whole existence was based on following a dream that she and her father had wanted for her. She wanted it for herself, desperately so, but she wanted it for him, too.'

'My real family thinks very little of me,' Leo said quietly. 'I am their hot-headed son who does not compare favourably to their older one in any aspect.'

'But...' How to make him see that he was so much more than his parents' blind assumptions about a man they must barely know. She had learned the hard way that you couldn't change how people perceived you once they had made up their own mind about you. If only she could make him see that, if not for her benefit, then at least to set him free from invisible ties that would restrain him for the rest of his life if he didn't cut himself loose.

He shook his head. 'I'm going to prove them wrong. They will see, when I am a member of the King's Knights, that I am just as worthy as him. I regret that I am unable to aid you, Ari, but you must see that it is impossible.'

And finally, she did. She was not just battling against his two friends but against Leo's deep-seated belief that achieving this great honour would make a difference to how his family viewed him. It didn't matter that it wouldn't; he would never stop trying.

At last, he looked up and met her gaze. She could see the anguish in his eyes and knew that he spoke the truth. He was miserable at the idea of her imminent marriage but he would do nothing to stop it happening. She should be angry but she finally understood. She really was on her own; she always had been. She had lost nothing because she'd never had anything to lose. And yet she couldn't help but feel that she had lost everything.

She turned away from him, fussing over Bel until the odd ache in her chest began to dim and the strange lump in her throat subsided.

Neither of them spoke as they climbed back onto their horses and began to follow the trail once more.

Chapter Thirteen

For a reason she couldn't fathom, Ari found it painful to watch Leo as he led the way throughout the rest of the afternoon. Instead, she focused on the undergrowth that lined their way. A fox ran alongside them for a while, flashes of red appearing through the thick leaves. Far above them, a bird of prey called.

'We are not going to reach the next village before nightfall,' Leo said eventually.

'How far is it?' Ari had been looking forward to stretching out on a large mattress. She didn't have it in her to attempt an escape tonight, not after that lengthy bout. She knew she should be worried about her lack of desire to get free, but she couldn't find the energy to care.

'I'm not sure but there is no sign that we're getting close.' He brought Bosco to a stop. 'Listen.'

No sounds reached her other than the rustling of the undergrowth and a blackbird's call.

'We'll have to camp out for tonight.'

She puffed out her cheeks and sighed loudly.

He laughed quietly. 'I know how you feel but we only have ourselves to blame. If we hadn't spent so long battling each other, we could be warming our toes in front of a fire while indulging in a rich stew. You could be contemplating how you're going to give me the slip, and I would be watching your overly expressive face for clues as to what you are plotting.'

Hmm, so that was how he kept catching her. She would have to bear her facial expressions in mind for her next attempt. She might not want to sleep in the woods but the situation did work in her favour. It delayed their arrival at the next place, which meant she could gather strength before her next escape effort.

Leo nudged Bosco off the path and she followed close behind. It was slow going but eventually they seemed to reach a spot that appealed to Leo. He leapt down from the stallion and stripped one of the bags off the horse's side. 'Will you see to the horses while I set this up?'

Ari nodded and set to her task while keeping an eye on what Leo was doing. He appeared to be creating some sort of makeshift shelter. When he was done, he stood up, brushing his hands together and giving the appearance of someone pleased with themselves.

'It's very small,' she said because it seemed she couldn't help but tease him, hoping that the banter would dispel the melancholy that had settled over them.

'I hadn't anticipated sharing it with a gently born lady,' he responded quickly because it seemed he couldn't help but needle her in return.

'I'm more than happy to sleep out under the stars.'

'I'm sure you are,' he said drily. 'But *you* will be in there and *I* will be outside.'

Her heart thudded in what couldn't be disappointment. She pressed her fingers to it.

'Is everything…?' He nodded to her hand. 'You look…'

'I'm fine.' She turned around and began to hunt through one of her packs, blindly looking for nothing because she'd realised that she was disappointed because he would not be joining her in the small space. Whatever happened, their time together was running out and she knew that she wanted to lie next to him again, to feel the length of his body pressed against hers if only while they slept. 'Fool,' she muttered to herself. 'You are a complete and utter fool.'

Leo may be the only man who respected her fighting skill, who made her laugh and whom she was coming to care for, but he was still a man. And men, she knew, let you down. Even her beloved father had done so in the end. He'd made her believe that she could have the life of a warrior but she was coming to believe that it was a fantasy. Ultimately, Leo was no different.

'Did you find what you're looking for? Because, if you're ready, I've got a fire going. I've nothing to go on it but I do have some of that honey bread you like so much.'

She closed the pack, not commenting on whether she'd found anything. It would have been hard to come up with an answer since she wasn't searching for anything.

He didn't question her as she sat down beside him, only handing her the bread. It was slightly stale today but still one of the better things she had ever tasted.

'I'm going to become a soldier,' she said after she'd finished the last bite.

'What?' He'd been staring into the flames, obviously not expecting her to speak.

'When I get away from you. I am not going to meet a lover or join a nunnery, I am going to become a soldier.'

He blinked at her, seemingly dumbfounded by her statement.

'I was to tell you what I was going to do when I got away from you if you won the bout earlier. You won and so I am telling you.'

'I see.' He swallowed. 'You are very skilled.' She couldn't help it, she glowed at his praise. 'But I think you will find it hard. I do not know of any female soldiers.'

'That is why I have cut my hair. I have no chest to speak of and under chainmail it will be completely unnoticeable. I can easily pass as a youth and... Why are you shaking your head?'

'You will never pass as a man.'

She bristled. 'I—'

He held up a hand to forestall her argument. 'This has nothing to do with your skill. You surpass many of the warriors I know.' Her father had always said so but she had begun to think his praise didn't count. Leo's words made her feel special again, even if it was part of a speech telling her what she didn't want to hear. 'You will not pass as a man because you are an exceptionally beautiful woman. Any man who even glimpses you will know you for what you are.'

Her mouth fell open; for once she was lost for words. No one had ever called her beautiful before. She had been called pretty once before, but the boy who had called her that had wanted to put his hands on her breasts, and she had been too busy kneeing him where it hurt to find out whether he really meant it.

Leo didn't seem to think he'd said anything remarkable; it was as if her beauty was common knowledge, which it wasn't. At least as far as she was concerned.

He leaned backwards, his broad back settling against a fallen tree. 'Have I finally found a way to get you to stop talking?'

'I'm not beautiful,' she managed. 'Lord Owain once told me I was a pale imitation of my mother and he was not wrong.'

'Lord Owain ap Llewellyn is a fool,' Leo growled.

'I'm not saying that to be modest. I have seen myself in a looking glass. I know all the features you'd hope to have on your face are there and generally in the right place but there is nothing special about them.'

'All your features are in the right place.' His eyes twinkled with amusement. 'I've never heard anyone describe themselves in quite that way before. Look—' he sat up abruptly '—you can trust me on this. Your features are…' He studied her face. 'I'm not the sort of knight who writes courtly love poetry, which is another reason Lord Ormand does not think highly of me, but if I were, you would move me to wax lyrical about the way you look.'

He leaned back and began studying the fire again.

'This is to put me off becoming a soldier, isn't it?' It had to be; there was no other reason for such lavish praise.

He frowned. 'No. Me throwing you over my shoulder and carrying you back to whichever place you have tried to escape from is to stop you becoming a soldier. I am only telling you the truth. Surely you are aware of the way men look at you as you walk past?'

'They never do.'

He bent his knee and propped his arm up on it. 'Perhaps it is just as well you are not going to become a soldier because you are not very observant.' He raised an eyebrow. 'Yesterday a man walked into a wall he was so busy staring at you.' He grimaced as if the thought gave him a bad taste in his mouth.

'I saw that and it was because you were growling at him.'

'I was growling because he was staring.'

She mulled over his comments. She did not think he was lying but he was mistaken. If she were beautiful then other men would have mentioned it to her before. 'Well, this is going to be one of the very many things you are wrong about.'

He laughed and she smiled. She wanted to keep talking about how attractive he found her but she knew that danger lay that way, and so she asked him about Bosco and how the stallion had come into his possession, and the rest of the evening passed in funny tales about him and his fellow knights. By the time darkness had fallen completely she found that her cheeks were aching from smiling so much.

Chapter Fourteen

The fire smouldered so low that Leo could no longer make out the features of Ari's face. Features she described as being *there* and features he found he could not stop staring at. He now knew that handing her over to Lord Cradoc was going to be the worst thing he had ever done in his whole life. Wasn't rescuing maidens part of his chivalric duty? His parents would be disappointed in him but he wasn't sure he cared anymore. It would nearly kill him to leave her and he knew that the marriage would destroy her spirit. It would be near to impossible to do and yet he had to. Every time his mind tried to formulate a plan in which he carried her away with him, he could never see it through to the end. There were too many obstacles. Everything led back to the knowledge that if he failed to be in Pembroke within the next week, he would have failed not only his mission but all the other aims in his life as well. Would his parents be more disappointed that he had failed in his duty or failed in doing what was honourable? He didn't know.

'Are you thinking of your responsibilities again?' Ari asked softly.

Surprised, he glanced at her. 'What makes you say that?'

'You have a tightness around your eyes sometimes. I have been wondering why but it showed itself intensely when you were talking about your family earlier. I've been thinking about what you told me, and I have an opinion, if you would like to hear it.'

'It won't change my mind about delivering you to your destination.'

She made a noise that sounded distinctly like an angry cat but he wisely kept that observation to himself.

'I don't expect it to. I only want you to think about what I say. Lord Owain wanted me to be a certain way and so I moulded myself into exactly what he wanted.'

'A young woman who wants to run away to become a soldier?'

'*He* doesn't know that. He thinks I am exactly as I present myself: a docile, pleasant young woman keen to become a wife. No matter how hard I tried, how rational my arguments, his opinion of me never changed.'

Leo tapped his foot with a long stick. 'You are saying my endeavours to impress my parents are pointless.'

She inhaled softly. 'That sounds brutal, but, yes, I suppose I am.'

'I see.' He could tell by the set of her shoulders that she wanted him to expand, but he had nothing else to say.

He stared at the fire, not seeing the flames but his mother, praising Alban for some small feat he had achieved, something that Leo could already do. He began to wonder if his obsession with proving himself worthy of their praise and their love was the wish of a child and not a man. Was Ari right?

'I think we should get some rest,' he said eventually. 'Tomorrow is going to be another long day of travelling.'

He heard her stand. 'Are you sure you don't want to join me in the shelter?' He was glad when she didn't push him to talk about his family anymore.

He paused. Yes, he did want to join her there, and that was why he wouldn't because his desire had nothing to do with shelter and all to do with the impulse to hold her in his arms as she slept. 'It would be too cramped. I will stay out here.'

He heard her mutter something under her breath, but it was too quiet for him to hear. She was shuffling around, obviously trying to find a way in, which would be next to impossible in the darkness. 'Need any help finding a way in?' he asked because he wanted to needle her, to engage, because every moment that they weren't felt like a waste.

'I am perfectly capable.' More fumbling sounded. He bit the inside of his cheek to stop himself from laughing.

'Ha!' she cried in triumph and moments later, she went still.

'Well done,' he murmured, because it seemed he couldn't help but tease her.

'You are such a—'

He waited for the inevitable insult but none came.

'I'm a...?'

'Shush, I'm asleep.'

He chuckled softly and they lapsed into silence.

He must have dozed off because he awoke to find water trickling down his face. He frowned as he wiped his skin, blinking as he struggled to wake up. A breeze ruffled the leaves above and more water dropped onto his face. It was raining, not heavily, but enough to make it uncomfortable.

He pulled his cloak tighter around himself and hunkered down in his spot. He closed his eyes but now that he was awake, he couldn't shake the feeling that he should check on Ari. Even though Bel was still tethered to a nearby tree, Leo knew that meant nothing. She could have decided to go without her; that had seemed to be her plan back in Carmarthen.

'Are you awake?' he whispered.

No reply.

His stomach turned over.

'Are you awake?' he asked again, louder this time.

'No,' came her belligerent return.

Relief coursed through him. 'Right. Of course you aren't. I apologise for disturbing you.'

He didn't say anything else. She was there and he could relax. He settled back against the tree trunk, gazing up at the sky. The rain was coming down a bit heavier now, dripping into his hair and running off the end of his nose.

'Is it raining?' Arianwen asked.

'A little.'

'It doesn't sound like a little.'

'That's the strange thing about tent fabric. It makes rain sound louder and heavier than it is.'

She sighed. 'Stop being stubborn and come and join me. I shan't ravish you, if that's what you are worried about.'

'As if I would worry about a thing like that.' It was the opposite, in fact; he was more concerned about what *he* would do if they were in close proximity again. Then again…if he was lying next to her, it would be far harder for her to escape, so he could relax and get some decent sleep. 'Fine. I will join you.'

He found the lip of fabric lying on the ground and

lifted it so that he could crawl into the space. The darkness beneath the fabric was absolute.

'Ouch.'

He snatched back his hand. He had no idea what he had just leant on but it had been soft.

'Again, I apologise,' he muttered. 'I'm not sure this is a good idea after all.'

'It will be fine.' A hand settled on his shoulder, the warmth of her touch coursing through him. 'Oh, you're wet.'

'I apologise,' he said for the third time, although he wasn't sure why. It wasn't his fault it was raining.

'No matter. With a little rearranging we will be comfortable and dry.'

Her hands fluttered at the opening on his cloak and he hissed in a breath.

She stilled. 'Did I hurt you?'

'No.' It was the opposite; her touch was almost unbearably good, even through the layer of fabric. 'What are you doing?'

'Rearranging us.'

'Do we need that?' he asked, even as his body thrilled as the backs of her fingers brushed his throat.

'Trust me.' She tugged his cloak off and he shivered as cold air rushed over him. 'Lie down.'

He slowly lay backwards, half expecting to hit his head on something, but the ground was soft beneath him. Something warm and soft settled over him, something that smelled of Arianwen and then something heavier.

'It's good that you can sometimes follow instructions,' came Arianwen's voice from somewhere near his feet.

'Only when it benefits me.' That wasn't true. Part of

being a good knight was obeying orders but he knew that was not what she wanted to hear. Like him, she seemed to want the light-hearted chatter that flowed between them because otherwise this moment would become too loaded, too tense. The soft material was tucked around his feet and legs. 'I don't think anyone has ever taken such good care of me,' he commented into the darkness.

'I'm used to having younger sisters to look after.'

He grinned but before he could formulate a teasing response, she slipped under the covers and curled up against his side. He froze.

'You're so cold,' she said, rubbing his arm. 'You should have come in here sooner.'

Her voice showed no sign that she was affected by his nearness at all, and yet he felt the touch of her hand on every bit of his body. He was hard, harder than he'd been that morning with her at the inn. He hadn't even taken any clothes off, for goodness' sake. All it had taken was the sounds of her pleasure and he'd been lost. Now it would seem that he didn't need either of those to make it happen even faster this time.

Her hand came across his chest and she was rubbing his other arm, muttering about foolish men and dire illnesses. He was losing a battle with himself, a battle she didn't even know was raging. He wanted to feel her in his arms again, to touch her, to hold her, to get her to make those sounds again.

'It's because you're not wearing enough clothes.'

'W…what?' His mind was shattered into a thousand pieces and he could make no sense of what she was speaking.

'You're cold because you're not wearing enough lay-ers. Why did you take your undergarments off this morning? It was not very good forward planning because now you are cold.'

'I…took them off because…um…when we…' How to explain without embarrassing himself once more.

'You are not making any sense. I can grasp more of an understanding from Bel.'

He laughed, he couldn't help himself. Her insult brought him back from the edge of desire. He cleared his throat. 'Do you know what happens between a man and a woman in order to make a baby?'

'Yes.'

'Hmm.'

'What does that ambiguous noise mean? I have slept in the Great Hall and have seen what happens between a man and a woman. There is no need to make patronising sounds.'

Laughter rumbled in his chest. 'Perhaps you should tell me what you know and then I will explain any missing information.'

'Why do I have to tell you?'

'Because if you knew everything, you would know why I am unable to carry on wearing my undergarments after this morning.'

Ari went very still.

'I can almost hear you thinking.'

'I'm trying to piece it together from what I already know, but you are not being very helpful.'

Her arm was still across his chest as if it was the most natural thing in the world for her to cuddle up to him. Without thinking about it too much, he brought his own hand up to cover hers. She snuggled closer and he wanted to stay in this moment for as long as possible, to shut out the world and just be with her.

A finger prodded his chest. 'You must tell me.'

He sighed; he was going to have to do this. 'When a man and a woman make a baby, some…there is… Hmm, this is harder than I thought to explain.' Absently, he rolled to his side, tucking her against him. She curled into his grip and his arm slid up the length of her back until his fingers reached the nape of her neck. He lightly massaged the skin there and she arched into him. It was exquisitely delicious torture.

'You know that a man and a woman must lie together to make a baby, yes?' She nodded against his chest. 'Did you know that a man must spill his seed into a woman?'

'No,' she mumbled against him.

He cleared his throat, his mouth uncommonly dry. 'If he does that outside of the body then there is…wetness.' Despite the comfortable position, this was so awful that the muscles in his spine crunched tightly. 'This morning, when we were, um, rubbing against each other, this happened to me. I couldn't walk around with the, um, *wetness* against my skin.

His skin was a fiery inferno. Never had he been more grateful for the darkness.

'I see. And does this happen every time?'

It helped that she sounded so practical. It meant he could get through this with some of his dignity intact. 'Every time, yes.'

'And does it feel good?'

His skin got hotter still. 'Yes.'

'I'm pleased because it was the loveliest thing that

has ever happened to me and it would be unfair if you hadn't enjoyed it, too.'

He was crushed, completely and utterly destroyed by her innocent statement. He was at a loss for words, unable to convey how much what had passed between them had somehow been the pinnacle of all his days. How, for the first time in his life, he was thinking about more than just the next sword fight or the next goal. How, if it was up to him, he would spend the rest of his days with her learning the ways of her body, making her laugh and watching her grow round with his baby. These wants and desires must stay buried deep inside him because they had the ability to destroy them both.

'It was the loveliest thing that has ever happened to me, too.' He didn't care that he sounded like a lovesick squire; he wanted her to know that the moment that had passed between them was special.

'Really?'

'Really.'

'Have you done that with someone before?'

'Yes.'

'Oh.' He felt her sag against his body and he couldn't bear that he had disappointed her. 'I've only experienced it once and I didn't enjoy it.' He'd never told anyone this before because he hadn't wanted to seem like less of a man.

'Why did you do it, if it was so awful?'

'I was young and foolish, I suppose. There was this feeling amongst the men of the castle that you were not a true man until you had lain with a woman, and it was common knowledge that I hadn't done it yet with anyone. There was a woman—she worked in Lord Ormand's kitchens—and she'd been married before but after her husband died she had made it clear that she didn't want to wed again. She seemed to be interested in me—she kept me the best food and would flirt with me as I walked past. Eventually, she made it clear exactly what she wanted from me and I thought, why not? I should never have agreed to it but I thought she liked me as a person... But what happened afterwards showed me that she didn't. It was not an enjoyable experience.'

He remembered the way she had led him to the woods behind the castle, how he had not felt any anticipation, only a sick sort of dread that he would somehow embarrass himself through his lack of experience. The situation had been worse than he'd expected but not for the reasons he'd imagined. She had groped him, hurting him more than pleasing him, but eventually things had worked and she had seemed to enjoy herself, breathing in his ear about how big and strong he was.

'It only happened the once. Afterwards, I was...uncomfortable about what had happened. I hadn't enjoyed it and I thought perhaps there was something wrong with me.'

The words were pouring out of him now, thoughts and feelings he'd kept to himself for so long spilling into the night. It was surprising how much he wanted to tell Ari and how much lighter he was already feeling from sharing his secrets.

'My humiliation didn't end there. I was the biggest warrior in the castle and she had taken my virginity. She told everyone. Going into detail about my manhood, and about things that should remain private. It took months for me to feel clean again. I have avoided women since then.'

'She sounds awful. I am sorry that you had that experience.'

'I am glad that I will have what we did this morning to remember forever.' Not only because it had been with Ari but also because it was a relief to find that he could feel desire, that being with another person could give him the joy that other men experienced. After his only other sexual encounter with a woman, he'd not been sure that he would be able to.

'Me, too.' His heart squeezed at her simple statement.

She lapsed into silence for a moment. 'When you said it was that pleasant all the time, how did you know if you've only done it the once and didn't enjoy it?'

He groaned and rested his head against her hair; it was as silky as it looked. 'Do I have to answer that question? Have I not embarrassed myself enough for one evening?'

'The answers are yes and no.'

He laughed. Even though he didn't want to tell her, he knew he would because he didn't seem to be able to stop himself. 'Ugh. Fine. I can make myself feel that way by doing something similar to what we did this morning.'

She was silent again but now he knew that was not necessarily a good indication that she was finished.

'Could *I* make myself feel that way?'

He squeezed his eyes shut but that did not stop the images flitting across his brain. He'd never seen her bare skin but he'd felt her through her clothes and he had a very good imagination when it came to her. Now he would live with the torture of imagining her touching herself and bringing herself pleasure forever.

'I suppose,' he ground out.

'How?'

Was she trying to kill him with these questions? Now all he could think about was his mouth on hers. It was doing nothing to alleviate his discomfort, which was now almost painful and incredibly insistent that Leo bury it deep in Arianwen until neither of them could talk or even walk.

'You'll have to figure it out for yourself.'

He could not take any more of this discussion. This morning he had embarrassed himself by how quickly her moving over him had brought him release. It would be even worse if she managed to do it just by talking to him. He was perilously close to it already.

Her fingers tapped his back. 'I have many questions.'

'I'm sure you do but now it is my turn to be asleep.'

He closed his eyes and pretended he was sleeping even though he knew that she knew that he wasn't.

'Fine, but don't think this is the end of this conversation forever.'

'It absolutely is.'

'It isn't.'

He didn't respond. She let out a contented sigh and turned her head so it was resting on his chest and, unbelievably, to his mind, fell almost instantly to sleep.

Leo lay there for an impossibly long time, trying and failing to accept that very soon, he was going to have to live without Arianwen in his life. He had no idea how he was to survive such a thing.

Chapter Fifteen

The sun crept higher in the sky, burning away the remains of last night's rain. The two horses plodded on, neither of their riders in much of a hurry to get anywhere. At least, Ari was in no mood to hasten their speed, and Leo seemed to feel the same. She knew why she was delaying their progress, although she was less sure why Leo was going slowly. She thought, hoped, it might be for similar reasons to her own: because he wanted to spend more time with her than the end of their journey allowed. She was sure he desired her as much as she did him. She could see it in his eyes and feel it in his response to her body but she was not sure whether he liked her as much as she liked him.

No matter how they moved, it did not change the fact that she was running out of time. In two days, they would reach their destination. She needed to get away from Leo before that happened. She needed to trick Leo somehow, to pretend that she was compliant and then run when she had the chance, but every time she came up with a plan she found a reason not to and it hurt. And that pain had nothing to do with her lack of opportunity and everything to do with how hurt he would be if she succeeded, because there was no getting away from the knowledge that for her to win, the man she had come to care for would have to fail.

A fly buzzed near her cheek and she swiped it away. As she turned, she caught sight of something in the trees to the side of them, something that shouldn't be there. She glanced at Leo. From the stiffness of his posture she guessed he had seen it, too. There was a crunch and her suspicions were confirmed; someone was following them in the undergrowth, and not subtly, either.

A thrill ran through her. All her training, all her years of waiting, had been leading up to something like this. This would finally be a chance to test out her skills for real, to see whether she was worthy of calling herself a soldier.

'Are you hungry?' Leo asked, leaning into one of his saddlebags.

They had stopped not long ago and eaten the last of their rations, and Ari knew he wasn't really talking about food but about what stalked them in the forest. Metal glinted in his hand, caught by the sun. If she hadn't been watching him intently, she wouldn't have noticed him slipping a short blade up his sleeve.

She shrugged, affecting nonchalance. 'I can eat if you want to or wait a little longer. What is your preference?'

His gaze flicked to the dense trees that lined the path.

'Perhaps a little longer and then we'll stop. Do you have anything with you?'

She felt her dagger strapped to her side. 'Yes, of course. I'm always hungry and keep food with me all the time.'

His eyes glinted with amusement. 'Excellent.'

They rode on in silence. Whoever had ridden up beside them in the trees had fallen back and now they were moving with more stealth, but the occasional burst of flight from birds disturbed by whomever was passing through confirmed that they were still being followed.

The path widened and she spurred Bel on to ride beside him. 'What do you think is happening?' she murmured.

'Three people at least,' he said softly, 'have been following us for a while. Possibly quite a few more. It's hard to tell as they are so far behind.'

'Why not rush at us now? What are they waiting for?'

'My guess is that they want to surround us in more open ground. That way all of them can be involved in the attack. The path is perhaps too narrow for them.'

'Either that or they know they will make too much noise as they pass us and then we will be ready for them.'

He nodded. 'It's probably both.' He grinned. 'Shall we make things trickier for them?'

She nodded, exhilaration pulsing through her. That Leo trusted her abilities thrilled and touched her in equal measure.

'Let's speed things up.' Leo nudged Bosco into a trot and then a canter as Bel followed. Behind them, Ari heard their pursuers increase their speed, too. They raced along, Ari's heart beating doubly quick.

They broke into an almost circular clearing and headed to one side of it. 'Let's stop and wait,' said Leo, whirling Bosco around so that he was facing the way they had come.

Riders burst into the space after them, coming to an abrupt halt when they saw Leo and Ari waiting for them. Seven, Ari counted. A large number but not insurmountable, not if she and Leo played this right. She'd witnessed Leo fight and knew that he was better than good and she was, too. They were outnumbered but that didn't mean they were going to come out of this encounter worse off than their opponents.

'Griffiths,' murmured Leo. 'How predictably annoying.'

Ari nodded in agreement. 'At least we know he's a bad fighter. The others don't look much better, either. We have a chance, don't you think?'

Leo slanted his gaze in her direction. 'I don't suppose I can persuade you to ride away from this?'

'I can look after myself. Do *you* want to ride away and let *me* deal with it?'

He barked out a laugh. 'I see your point. I believe we have more than a chance but we must not be overconfident. There are more of them than there are of us.'

'I can count,' she said acerbically.

Leo called across the clearing, 'What do you want?'

'You did not show me enough respect at our last meeting,' Griffiths sneered.

Leo rolled his eyes and Ari pressed her lips together to stop herself from laughing. How she was finding merriment in this situation she did not know. This was not playing at swords, this was a real contest and she had never fought for her life before. She would do well to take it seriously and yet exhilaration was flooding through her veins.

'In return for your disrespect, I want the girl.'

Ari glanced down at herself. The only thing of value she wore was the clasp on her cloak. She doubted it had much value but, even so, she was not about to give it up. Unless he wanted…

'Does he want me because…he wants to bed me?' She shuddered.

Leo nodded, his lips thin. 'I will die before I allow that to happen,' Leo snarled. 'Griffiths, I thought we made our position perfectly clear in Carmarthen. You are not a strong fighter. If you engage the lady and me in a fight, you will lose, even with the six other men you have brought with you.'

The men behind Griffiths sniggered and Ari's fist curled.

'You may think yourself a good fighter but you are vastly outnumbered,' Griffiths countered. 'Give me the girl and your horses and then nobody needs to fight and you won't get hurt.'

'You're not getting the girl,' Leo stated flatly.

'The *woman*,' Ari countered, heartily sick of being called a girl, 'can speak for herself and I am not coming with you.'

'Very well,' said Griffiths, seeming pleased with their response.

It was a fight he had wanted all along. He wanted to teach them that he was not to be messed with. Hopefully, Leo and Ari would show him the error of his ways.

'Men!' roared Griffiths. 'Bring me the girl. I do not care what happens to the man.'

Like the coward he was, Griffiths held back as the rest of the group moved forward.

'You take the left,' Leo ordered. 'I'll take the right.'

Pride surged through her. Leo had not been paying lip service when he had complimented her on her skills. He truly believed she could defend herself. Ari surged forward, the call of the battle strong within her, her focus narrowing on her opponents. The men had clearly not expected to be attacked by a woman and had not even drawn their swords by the time she reached them. With a quick nudge, she was able to dislodge one from his horse. She whirled around, bringing Bel to face him. He was staggering to his feet, clearly dazed. She charged at him again, hitting him with the flat side of her blade. He went down and stayed there.

Out of the threesome on the left, one was staring at her open-mouthed and the other was pulling his sword from its scabbard. Guessing she had time to deal with the shocked one later, she turned towards the one who almost had his wits about him. She rushed towards him, yelling to create confusion. He kept his seat but his parry with his blade was weak, and she wasn't worried he would be a decent opponent. She came at him again. Grabbing the reins of his horse, she managed to get the beast running before she let go and rode away. Watching the man try to get his mount under control while swearing at her was almost amusing. She turned to the third man, who'd now managed to get his sword out. She needed a weapon, she realised; her dagger was not going to work against these longer blades. She jumped down from Bel, patting her on the rump to get her to move away from the danger.

'Good girl,' she murmured as the horse obeyed her instructions.

She ran to where the fallen man was, noticing that Leo had already dispatched one man, too. She pulled the sword from the prone body and waved it about.

It was of inferior quality and her father would not have allowed it near any of his men, but it would do in this tight spot. She surged to her feet. The two men she was fighting had now dismounted and she could hear Griffiths shouting instructions to them. She ignored him. What Griffiths wanted to do to her body was irrelevant and was not going to affect how she defended herself now. He was not going to get near her in order to do the vile things he was threatening. She knew that even if she failed, which she wouldn't, Leo would not allow Griffiths to so much as touch a strand of her hair. She paused, mid-step, her sword held high as she realised she trusted Leo completely and utterly. He was a man of his word and if he said he would do something, he would. He was the first man she had felt this way about since her father had died and the irony was not lost on her. He had said that he would deliver her to Lord Cradoc and so he would. Being a man of his word in this instance would not save her, no matter how he might feel about her.

She glanced across at him. He was down to one man, while she had two left. She needed to sort that out because, trustworthy though he may be, Leo would also be unbearably smug if he did better than her. She set to work. It was not long before she only had one opponent left, too.

'My advice to you,' she called to the remaining man, the one who had been shocked earlier, 'is to run. My friend and I—' she waved her purloined sword at Leo '—we have no quarrel with you but we will beat you if you remain.'

She could see the hesitation in his eyes and knew she was winning. 'Did Griffiths offer to pay you? Because you should know he doesn't pay what he owes. I've witnessed him reneging on a deal before. It's one of the reasons he wants to get revenge on me.'

'Don't listen to the witch,' snarled Griffiths, coming closer.

'If I'm a witch, why do you want me so badly?'

Griffiths smirked. 'You have a pretty enough face. I figure I can make some money out of you. Once you've opened your legs a time or two, you'll soon lose your swagger and maybe—' Griffiths never finished whatever he was about to say because Leo flew at him, pulling Griffiths off his horse and sending him sprawling to the ground.

Ari turned away for a moment, scanning the area for her last opponent, but he must have taken advantage of Griffiths's distraction to run away because there was no sign of him or his horse. She crossed the rest of the small clearing. The last of the men were in various states of consciousness but all of them would live. By the time she'd finished her inspection, Griffiths was cowering on the floor in front of Leo, who was holding the tip of his sword to the man's throat.

'Could you fetch me some rope?' Leo asked her as she approached. He nodded towards Griffiths's horse. She made her way over to it and found a coil of rope strapped to the back. She unhooked it and brought it back to Leo.

'Was this for me?' she asked, holding it up for Griffiths to see.

He only whimpered in response. Ari caught Leo's ferocious glare and understood why Griffiths was too scared to answer. Leo looked as if he could kill whole armies, his huge body coiled to strike. She handed the binding over to Leo and watched as he roughly tied Griffiths up.

'You're lucky,' Leo growled, addressing Griffiths, 'that we have to be on our way and I don't have time to see to you properly. If you turn out to be luckier still, these men will unbind you when they wake up, although I hope they leave you here to rot. Don't come after us because if I see you again, I *will* kill you first and then ask questions. Are we clear?' Griffiths nodded, all his bravado gone in the swiftness of his defeat. 'Good.'

Leo turned to Ari, his eyes still full of fire. 'Let's go.'

They gathered their horses and rode off, not once turning around to look at the men they had defeated.

They rode hard for several leagues, finally coming to a stop when a small settlement came into sight.

'Did you see Griffiths's face? I thought he was going to cry!' said Ari.

Leo turned towards her. 'You sound...'

'Happy?' she finished for him.

'Yes, happy. Aren't you scared or angry? I could tear down mountains I'm so furious.' His eyes were still blazing despite the many leagues they had travelled.

'Are you serious? That was the most fun I've had in ages.'

'Fun! Did you not hear what Griffiths planned to do to you? I should...' Leo tugged on the reins as if he was going to go back and finish off what he had started.

'I did hear but I was never in any doubt that we would prevail. We had them dispatched in mere moments.'

He stared at her as if she had sprouted a second head. 'Moments! Ari, it took most of the afternoon.'

She snorted. 'It did not. It was already past midday

when we started and we've been riding for some time and it is still not evening. Look.' She gestured to the sky, which was turning a lovely shade of pink.

He was shaking his head. 'You are a strange person.'

That stung. 'Because I am a woman who enjoys a fight?' She had thought that Leo was different, that he did not see her sex as an impediment. 'You think, like Lord Owain, that a woman should not fight? Because I thought you were different. I thought…'

He shook his head more firmly. 'No, that's not it at all. The way you fight is a thing of beauty. No, I mentioned the word *strange* because, aside from myself, I have never seen anyone who enjoyed combat more. You did not seem as if you were afraid at any point.'

Ari thought for a moment. 'If I had been by myself, I would have been scared because they would have outnumbered me and I could not have dealt with seven men at once. But I know how good a fighter you are and I know my skill level. There was not one moment where I thought we would be bested.'

He turned back to face the village, opened his mouth and then closed it again.

'What is it?' she prompted.

He let out a long breath. 'I was scared.'

Ari nearly fell off her horse. 'You were?'

'Yes.' He let out a long breath. 'I've never experienced terror in a fight before but today, today I felt real fear.' He tapped his chest. 'Right here.'

She was incredulous. He had been a powerful force to be reckoned with. Not one of those men had stood a chance against him as his sword had whirled and slashed through the air. 'But they were a bunch of ragtag misfits!

Griffiths probably hired them because they were desperate to earn a few coins. They never stood a chance against you. I don't want to add to your supreme confidence but you probably could have handled them by yourself.'

'I know all that. I have eyes. I knew they were not worthy opponents and yet I still felt a desperate fear for the first time in my life.'

'Why?' She was completely baffled. She had not thought it possible that he would feel such an emotion during a short skirmish like that. It was barely worth talking about.

'Because of you.' His eyes were anguished.

'But I told you, I was fine.'

'I know you were. I saw you, Ari. You are one of the greatest fighters I have ever seen. Your flexibility, your strength and your total disregard for your own safety make you formidable.' She glowed at his praise. She'd never been called formidable before—good and passable, but never anything higher. And for the past few years, she'd only practised in the privacy of her chamber or hidden deep in the woods that surrounded her stepfather's castle, as if her abilities were something of which to be ashamed. His words healed a part of her she hadn't even realised was broken.

'The thing is, Ari,' Leo continued, sounding no happier, 'I believed what Griffiths was saying to you. If he had got his hands on you, he would have done all those things and then let others do it to you and I…' He shook his head as his words failed him.

She reached across and touched his arm. She didn't want to see this sad version of him, not in their last hours together. 'He never would have got to me, Leo.'

'Hmm.'

They rode their horses slowly for a little way in silence until he finally said, 'At least you have to agree with me now that you look nothing like a man.'

'Why on earth would I agree with you about that?' She was pleased to hear the teasing note back in his voice even if she didn't like what he was saying.

'Those men were not fooled by your disguise.'

'But I am still wearing women's clothing. You wait until I am in a man's surcoat. You won't recognise me.'

He laughed darkly. 'Ari, I would know you anywhere. Right now, I'd know that smell anywhere.'

He wrinkled his nose and she gasped in mock outrage. 'You're one to talk. You look like you've spent a few days in a pigsty.'

'You look like you've bathed in a swamp.' His eyes were twinkling again and her heart surged.

The rest of the journey passed in a competition to come up with the most imaginative ways to describe how bad they both smelled. Ari was grateful for it. The haunted look in Leo's eyes had scared her more than any battle ever could, although she wasn't sure why.

Chapter Sixteen

There was only one inn in the small market town they came across towards the end of the day. Whether they would share a chamber or not wasn't discussed. Leo only requested one and they traipsed up the stairs together.

'I'll fetch up some water,' he murmured before disappearing once more. She glanced at the open doorway. He had left her alone, seeming to trust that she wouldn't try to escape, and he was right. Despite this being an opportunity to try to get away from him, she had no inclination to do so. It was foolish but there it was. She could argue it was because she would not get far. Both she and Bel were exhausted from their efforts today, and she would not be able to run if Leo was chasing her. But that was not the reason she would not leave and that worried her. She did not leave because she wanted to be with Leo for one last night. Tomorrow she would start her new life, but tonight she would spend with him.

The straw mattress looked tempting but she wasn't about to flop on it. Not when she was covered in sweat and mud and other bits of grime she didn't want to think about too much. She settled on a wooden chair and stared at the unlit fire.

Her heart leapt awkwardly when she heard Leo's heavy tread on the stairs. He stepped through the doorway with two large buckets of steaming water. 'They didn't have a tub I could fill, so we will have to make do with these.' He placed the water at the foot of the bed.

There was a gentle knock on the door. Leo moved towards it and Ari heard a murmured conversation about soap. Leo came back in carrying some cloths and a block he was sniffing. 'It smells better than it looks. I think there might be lavender in it.'

He held it out to her, and she took the oily square from him and sniffed. 'You're right. It does smell good but maybe that's because you smell like you've rolled in a filthy stable.'

He smiled and then glanced at the buckets before shuffling awkwardly on his feet. 'Would you like some privacy?' His gaze flicked to her, to the bed and then to the door.

Her heart beat painfully fast. She supposed she should say yes, that she did want to be alone while she bathed, but she didn't want to. She wanted him here and she wanted to see all of him, not just the back she had glimpsed yesterday. 'I'd like you to stay,' she said. 'That is, if you want to.' She didn't want to force him into a situation that made him uncomfortable.

He took a painfully long time to answer and when he did, his voice was hoarse. 'I want to, more than is perhaps healthy.'

She nodded as relief and something else potent rushed through her. 'Me, too.' She didn't know what the days that followed would bring but she did know that she could have this moment for herself, a space in time where she could gaze her full at this man, to perhaps touch him and map the contours of his body, learning what gave him pleasure, knowledge she would take into her new life.

Slowly, she went to the clasp of her tunic and undid it. The garment fell softly to the floor as she shrugged out of it. Leo swallowed as he copied her movements.

Ari's entire existence focused in on this chamber, the only sounds the swish of fabrics falling to the floor, the occasional thud as something heavier followed it and their heavy breathing, almost as if the pair of them had been running for days and had only now stopped.

And then Leo stood before her, all his clothes removed as she tugged the last of her undergarments off. He grunted but made no move towards her. She took her time in a lazy perusal of his body. She observed the wide shoulders and corded muscles of his arms, his thick chest covered with a sprinkling of dark hair, narrowed to a tapered waist banded with yet more muscle, his length, jutting out in front of him and then his thighs, thick and strong. She returned her gaze to his face. His eyes were glazed, his lips slightly parted. She had never seen anything so powerfully beautiful.

She stepped towards him and saw his fingers tremble. Something hot and possessive burned through her. He was hers, now and forever, no matter what happened next.

'Turn around,' she commanded, her voice thick, almost unrecognisable.

He did as she instructed without question. She leaned over and dipped a cloth into one of the buckets; the water was deliciously warm. She spread the soap over the wet cloth and stood tall.

Leo shivered as the cloth passed over his wide shoulders but she didn't think that had anything to do with the temperature. She took her time, gliding the cloth down one arm and then the other, leaving a soapy trail on his skin. She massaged it in, her fingers gliding over his muscles, and he grunted in pleasure. She washed the soap away and began moving down the length of his back until she reached the base of his spine.

'So good,' he murmured, his words slurred as she kneaded the muscles there, her fingers digging into his flesh.

She passed down the length of his leg and then the other, noting that his fists were tightly clenched.

She wanted to seem in control but her voice shook as she said, 'Turn around.'

A light smile touched the edges of his lips but his eyes were burning. She thought he might reach out to her then but he didn't, letting her take the lead in whatever this was.

She ran the cloth over his collarbone, the water pooling at the base of his throat. She touched it with the tip of her finger and he swallowed.

She worked her way along the hard planes of his stomach, not touching his hardness, which seemed to strain towards her. His knees were locked as though he was exerting great effort to keep himself standing. She worked her way up and down his legs before dropping the cloth back into the water. She wanted to explore the remaining part of him without fabric in the way. She rubbed the soap over her hands until they were slick and then she slid her fingers along his length. He inhaled sharply and she caught his gaze. He was looking at her as if she was his everything. Her heart swelled almost painfully.

Her hand moved up and down his length, slowly imitating the movement that had felt so good the previous day, her eyes locked on his face, not wanting to miss his reaction to her touch. He moaned. His lids were half-closed but his attention was fixed on her.

She stretched and lightly brushed his lips with her own. His lips moved in response, capturing hers. They moved together, their breath intermingling, learning what was good. His tongue touched her bottom lip and she jumped.

'Too much?' he murmured, his mouth brushing across her forehead, her eyelids, the edge of her jaw.

'Unexpected,' she replied.

She felt his smile against her cheek. 'For me, too.' His lips skimmed hers again. 'I am desperate to taste you.' His words seemed to light a fire within her and she moved her hand quicker, his hips thrusting in response. Now that he'd mentioned it, she was desperate to taste him, too. She pressed her mouth against his once more, but this time he pulled back.

'Now it's my turn to get you clean.'

She stopped moving, her hand still encircling him. 'Are you not enjoying…?' She glanced down between their bodies.

'More than you can imagine.' His hand covered hers and he moved it up and down over himself, his breath hissing out of him. 'But I cannot not touch you anymore. I need…' His voice held a rough, desperate edge. 'I need it to be my turn.'

He released his grip on her. Reluctantly, she let go of him and stepped back slightly. His eyes gleamed in triumph and delight. 'It's your turn to turn around.'

Her fingers trembled as she did what he ordered. The first pass of the warm cloth on her back was exquisite. The second had her moaning out loud. He pressed a kiss to her shoulder and she thought she might die from pleasure as his beard tickled her sensitive skin. Everywhere the cloth went, his mouth followed, kissing, licking, biting until she was quivering with need.

When he turned her to face him, she didn't wait. She pressed her mouth to his, opening to him until their tongues warred. He pulled her flush against him, his hardness against her stomach.

He lifted his head, his lips coming off hers in a moan. 'You're still not clean.' His voice sounded as if he had drunk many ales.

She shook her head. 'I cannot take any more.' She tried to reach for him but he turned his head away.

'You tortured me with this,' he ground out. 'Now it is your turn.'

'Torture?'

He smiled wickedly. 'You have no idea how hard it was to hold still and not touch you. Now you can try it. Be good.'

She whimpered as he dragged down her arm, across her collarbone and down the other. By the time he was tracing the curve of her breast she was begging him, for what exactly she wasn't sure, because her words were incoherent even to her. The first touch of the cloth to her sensitive nipples had her reaching out and gripping his forearm. 'I can't,' she whimpered. 'It's too much.'

'What, this?' he murmured, brushing over them again.

Her grip tightened, her fingers pressing into his muscles.

He swirled around both breasts, dipping the cloth between the centre and round before going back to her nipples, covering every piece of skin. An ache was building at her centre, an ache that craved his touch. She needed him, needed to feel him against her, to make her feel the way she had yesterday, but he seemed in no hurry to get there, moving down to wash over the length of her legs, avoiding the sensitive skin between them until she was nearly sobbing. Finally, when she thought she could take no more, he was touching her there. The pleasure was like nothing else as her world centred on that point.

She cried out, the wetness of the cloth mixing with her own. Then the cloth was gone and it was his hand exploring her, the delicious friction driving her wild until she could take it no more. She caught his mouth with hers and this time he did not pull away. She wrapped her hand around him and began to stroke again, matching the movements he made with his own hand, his muffled groans urging her on.

Somehow, they stumbled to the bed, their movements desperate, frantic, clumsy but always deliciously wonderful. And then she was crying out as waves of pleasure spiked through her and he was spilling onto her stomach, the warmth of him increasing the intensity of the moment.

As the world-changing sensations finally ebbed away, Leo dragged his mouth against the length of her jaw, settling his forehead against her neck, his hand still resting at the juncture between her thighs.

'I think I might have died,' he murmured into her skin.

She managed a weak chuckle. She was completely boneless, lost to this moment of perfection. 'Kissing...' she murmured, unsure of how to get across to him how much she had enjoyed the feeling of his mouth on hers.

'Kissing you is everything.'

She turned her lips to his forehead, pressing a soft kiss to his skin, hoping this conveyed that she felt the exact same way.

'I need to...' He shifted and, with what seemed like a momentous effort, pushed himself off the bed away from her. Cold air rushed over her and she immediately missed the feel of his body against hers.

Then he was back, wiping her stomach clean before returning to bed and dragging them both up to the top. He settled her body against his and wrapped his big arms around her. Her last thoughts before they fell into a dreamless sleep were, how on earth was she meant to live without him when the time came?

Chapter Seventeen

Leo woke as the morning light hit his face. They'd forgotten to close the shutters last night and the whole room was bathed in the golden sunshine that was unique to summertime. His arms were wrapped tightly around Ari as they had been when he'd fallen asleep; even in sleep he didn't want to let her go. He gently ran his fingers through her hair, watching the way the sunlight caught the ginger streaks within, flashing brightly as it fell softly back to her shoulder.

Before yesterday, he had never kissed a woman like this, and now all he wanted to do was trace her body with his lips. Before he could talk himself out of it, he was kissing the soft swell of her breast, and by the time he reached her taut nipple, her fingers were threading into his hair. His tongue traced the bud and her fingernails scraped against his scalp. He'd learned that the harder she gripped him, the more she muttered jumbled words of encouragement, writhing next to him as she lost control. He bit down lightly and she pulled at his hair, the bittersweet pain sending a jolt straight to his groin. He moved to her other breast, giving it the same treatment.

Her nails scratched over his scalp before raking down his neck and digging into his shoulder.

He moved down her body, pressing open-mouthed kisses to her stomach until he reached her soft curls. He had never kissed a woman here and had no real idea of what to do; he had only heard other men talk about doing so. Revolting as it had always sounded to him, he now couldn't think of anything he wanted to do more.

He was learning Ari's body and from the way she was gripping him, he knew she was loving this as much as he was. He was confident she would tell him if she hated what he was doing. One lick and she was arching off the bed, crying out and pressing into him. He pinned her to the mattress, his arm across her stomach making her whimper in a way that had him groaning into her. He discovered the small bud that seemed to make her senseless and he teased it with lips, tongue and teeth. She was bucking off the bed even as her fingers gripped his head, holding him in place. In this moment, he was a king. He found her opening, slowly, and gently pushed a finger into her, taking care not to go too fast or hard. This was new to her, new to him, and he did not want to hurt her. He pulled out when he feared he would cause her pain.

'No,' she cried. 'More.'

His soul triumphed, knowing she was as lost to this as he was. He entered her again, moving quicker now as her hips flexed to meet him, the noises she was making urging him on until she cried out, her release fluttering around him, and it was the most beautiful thing he had ever felt. She yanked on his hair to the point of pain and he felt his own release building within him. He stayed with her, licking and stroking until all her tremors had ebbed away. Then he was moving up her body and she was reaching for him blindly. She took him in her hand, stroked, once, twice and then he was spilling into the sheets, his head buried against her chest.

Slowly, he came back to himself. He was half lying on her, half off. There was a light sheen of sweat across the skin of her chest and he resisted the urge to lick it off.

'That was a lovely way to start the day,' she said, running her fingers through his hair, gently now but no less exquisite.

'It was perfect,' he replied, placing an absurdly chaste kiss to the side of her breast.

'They're very small,' she said, poking at one with her fingertip.

'Stop looking for compliments.'

She shook with laughter, her breasts moving in a delightful way that had him stirring again, which surely was impossible so soon after the last time. 'I'm not.' She took a small breath. 'I suppose I'm wondering why you seemed so enamoured with them.'

He reached across and cupped one with his hand, his thumb grazing her nipple. 'They are exactly the right size to fit inside my hand.' He squeezed and she sighed happily.

'I'm glad.'

He kissed her skin again and then the skin of her neck and then her mouth. Kissing anyone else would be a chore but with Ari it was what he was born to do.

Her stomach growled and he lifted his head. 'You're hungry.'

'Not really,' she said, pulling his mouth back to hers.

But now he was aware of it, he could hear the way her stomach grumbled. They had fought yesterday in a battle that had drained both of their energy and had not eaten in the evening, falling into bed together instead. She must be more than hungry and he could not bear that.

He pushed himself up to his elbows. 'I will go and fetch us something to eat.'

'No, stay for a while.' And then she was kissing him again, skimming his hardness with the back of her hand and he lost all reasonable thought.

It was some time later before he found the willpower to extricate himself from her arms, but he finally managed to stand so that he was gazing down at her. She was splayed before him like the most sumptuous feast. He could take her now, and she would welcome him, he knew. He could make her his in every way possible. If she was heavy with his child then no other man could stake a claim. She would be his forever. The urge within him was primal and hot, and yet there were so many things wrong with that idea that he knew he had to get away from her before he did something so incredibly foolish that there would be no way back from it. He had to be able to think clearly, to look at the situation from every angle and to bring himself back to the focus of his mission, to decide what it was he really wanted from his future. Ever since he had begun to consider that Ari might be right about him never being able to change his family's opinion of him, the thought had taken root. He wanted to think about it without her intoxicating presence. He stepped back from the bed, his body almost screaming at him to return to her.

Quickly, he splashed water on himself before pulling on his clothes. 'I'll be back shortly.' He glanced at her. 'Don't move at all.' He pointed a finger at her to emphasise the message and she grinned. His heart skittered and he was more than glad that she could not read his mind.

He was in trouble—worse trouble than he'd ever been in before. This made the disaster of the damaged manuscript and the subsequent half banishment seem like a small bump in the road. Now he had a simple but tortuous decision to make: complete his mission and fulfil his vow, destroying the happiness of the woman he loved, or help Ari escape the marriage arranged for her, betraying his friends and further disappointing his parents in the process. Because he did love her, of that he was sure. The choice was agonising and impossible.

Leo stumbled out of the tavern and sucked in a deep breath. The cool morning air filled his lungs but did not help with the torment in his mind. He knew he should not be leaving Ari alone, that to do so meant that she would probably escape from him. Indeed, if she were to do so then he would no longer have to make the impossible choice, but this was a weakness and he despised himself for it. But then, she might want to stay with him as much as he wanted to be with her. Perhaps she would wait and they could talk and maybe, just maybe, there was something they could do, something that would make it possible for them to be together.

He followed the smell of bread to a baker's, every step feeling as if chains were weighing him down, making his steps heavy and uncomfortable. No matter which way he looked at the situation he was in, he could not let down the two men who were counting on him. But he also could not hand over Ari to a man she did not want to marry and a life that would destroy the very essence of who she was. He was in an impossible place.

The two choices before him were diametrically opposed. He wished she would run away again, so far and so fast this time that it would be impossible to find her and then the choice would be made for him. But there he was again with the coward's way out and he was not one of those. The thoughts kept circling in his mind and he could not escape.

He must do something. He had to choose. He rubbed a hand down his face. But should he break his vow or her heart?

For now, he would focus on getting them something to eat. *That* he could do.

He joined a queue, awaiting his turn. In front of him, the townsfolk chattered in Welsh. It had been so long since he had learned the ancient language that he couldn't follow what was being said, and it was too much effort for him to even try. It was only when he heard the name 'Lord Cradoc' that he stood up straighter. Frustratingly, he could only work out fragments of the conversation. He caught *riders* and *bride*. There seemed to be a general air of excitement but there was nothing he could hold on to. Did the townsfolk know who Ari was? If they knew that Lord Cradoc's bride had spent the night in their small town… The blood drained from his face as he considered the implications. He and Ari had not been discreet during the night. Ari had been particularly vocal as he'd brought her pleasure. He hadn't thought to be quiet either; hell, he couldn't even remember what sort of noises he'd made but his throat felt hoarse, as if he had been shouting. Fear clutched at his heart. If word got to Lord Cradoc that his future bride had been with another man then the two of them would have more to worry about than choosing which path to follow. He glanced around at the strangers. The mood was not one of anger or even joyful anticipation of someone's downfall. It seemed…hopeful, he thought, almost as if the people were looking forward to something good. He wanted to turn back and run to her, to check she was safe and to get her far away, but until he knew the extent of the threat or even if there was one then he should stay where he was.

He reached the front of the queue none the wiser. 'You're new round here,' said the baker, thankfully in English.

'Aye,' croaked Leo.

'Anything to do with the news?'

'The news?'

'Lord Cradoc is to take a new bride. Fair beautiful, she's said to be and there's rumours she arrived in our town last night. Someone described her as a heavenly vision. I hope it's true. It will be good to have some young blood in that family and bring some life to the cantankerous old bastard. It will do him, and us, good if he has a pretty wife to warm his bed at night.' The baker laughed. 'There's hope he'll be so busy making his desperately needed heirs that he'll forget about us townsfolk and leave us in peace for a year or two.'

Leo made a strangled noise, which neither confirmed nor denied anything. His stomach was turning over. He could not imagine the beautiful, endlessly fascinating, always amusing Ari wedded to a quarrelsome old man. She had already escaped from a man who had tried to break her spirit; she would not survive being married to a man who would do the same.

'Lord Cradoc must be getting impatient about how long it's taking her to get here. Dewi said he saw riders leaving the castle this morning. There was a huge train of them with a wagon and everything. He thinks they must be on their way to meet her. Did you see the Lady Arianwen on the road?'

For a moment, Leo froze, unable to respond to the question or even move. Men were coming for Ari. She could already be gone, taken from the inn or escaping of her own accord and he was standing there, gawping at the baker. And then he was turning and sprinting back to the inn, his heart pumping wildly. He had to get to her, had to warn her, had to tell her how he felt, and he had to get her to help him plan a way for them both to escape. She'd have a good idea. She was resourceful and clever and…and he was wasting time.

He took the stairs two at a time and burst through the door into the chamber. It was empty.

Ari watched from the shadows as Leo sprinted past her as though the hounds of hell were after him. She couldn't swallow past the thick lump in her throat. She wanted to call out to him but she needed a moment away from his overwhelming presence, a moment to think, a moment to make the biggest decision of her life. She was finally unfettered. Leo did not know where she was, nobody did. She could slip into the woodland behind her and no one would be any the wiser. It would be so simple, in the end. But was she really free? Her heart certainly wasn't. It now belonged to somebody else and if she took what she wanted, her love for Leo would be pointless.

She clutched her small bag to her chest; there was

very little in it—some oatcakes, a few coins and her dagger. It had come with her everywhere so far and today was no exception, although she was still not sure what her next move would be. She could no longer pretend to herself that what happened to Leo after all this was over was of no concern to her.

If Leo didn't complete his mission successfully then he would let down his friends and break the vow he had made. Could she run knowing what her disappearance would cost the man she had come to love?

Ari leaned against the rough brick wall of the inn. Did she even have a choice? She knew that she loved Leo, had loved him for days now. She could not live with herself if she destroyed his chance at happiness, and the only way to do that was to sacrifice her own dreams of becoming a warrior for his. Finally, she understood why her father had left Windsor to be with her mother. He hadn't had a choice, either. Love was like that, it seemed. It put the needs of the other person above your own. It made you want them to be happy even knowing what it would mean for yourself. If she knowingly destroyed Leo's future, then her own freedom would not be worth having. She would not be able to live with herself knowing what she had done. So she would marry and tie herself to a man she didn't want, and she would do so willingly for Leo's sake.

She pushed herself off the wall and moved into the depths of the narrow alleyway. She just needed to collect herself before she saw him again. She would not cry in front of him. He must never know how hard this decision hit her, must never know that her heart was breaking, both because of the loss of her own future but also because she would likely never see him again. Angrily, she swiped at the tears that had escaped and were running down her face. Crying was pointless; she had learned that after the death of her father. It hadn't brought him back and it hadn't altered the new course of her life. She had vowed to herself that she would never indulge in them again and yet they did not stop falling now. She pulled her dagger from her bag. She concentrated on the ornate handle and on regulating her breathing. It had been a gift from her father many years ago, and tracing the intricate pattern calmed her. As the tears stopped, she worked through a drill and then another until her breathing was coming easier and she had come back to herself.

She would be able to face Leo now with a calmness she didn't feel inside. She turned to go, and as she made her way towards the light, the gallop of many hoofbeats sounded outside the inn. She froze, everything inside her telling her that this noise boded ill despite the laughter. Many voices sounded at once, and there was an air of excitement and celebration as if it was coming from a group of men returning from a successful hunt.

Then the light at the end of the tunnel was blocked by a large shape, a shape she instantly recognised.

'Leo,' she called out softly.

He turned and stared towards her, his face, shadowed as it was, impossible to read. He tilted his head in acknowledgement and then he was turning away from her without saying a word.

Ice crept down her spine, tingling into her fingers. She had only felt fear once, when she'd heard that her father might have died while out riding, and although it had taken days for him to pass, the fear had stayed with her the whole time. This was the exact same feeling.

She moved along the alleyway towards the end, keeping to the shadows. If Leo was in trouble then she would back him up, would fight with him until there was no breath left in her body. But as she got closer, she could hear only sounds of laughter, not of threat. Why, then, had he not called her over? Dread settled in her stomach, twisting and turning like a live serpent.

'Good morn, sir.' Someone was addressing Leo. She could make out his nod in return but he didn't appear to speak. 'I am Sir Timor from the house of Lord Cradoc. We have heard word that the Lady Arianwen has been seen riding towards this town and we have arrived to escort her to her new home. Have you seen her, perchance?'

Sweat coated Ari's palms. She was out of time. This was it, but Leo was still not saying anything. Her fingers sought out the wall, scrabbling for purchase, but she could get no hold on the rough surface. She'd made her decision but she hadn't expected to have to face it so soon. And then she heard Leo's voice. 'I have not seen her.'

The world stilled. He *had* seen her in this hiding place. He'd nodded to her only moments ago. He was lying for her, hiding her away so that she didn't have to go with them, and her heart thrilled at the knowledge. When it came to the critical point, he had sided with her, had chosen her instead of his two friends. It was the first time in her life that she had ever come first with anyone. Not even her beloved father had made her feel so special.

It made her decision on what to do easy.

She inhaled deeply, pushing herself upright. For years,

she had pretended to be someone she wasn't, had acted in a way that did not irritate her stepfather or upset her mother. The knowledge that she would have to live with Lord Cradoc in the exact same way, that he could never know what she really thought, had her walking the final steps along the alleyway. She had lived like it once, she could do it again.

She stepped into the small courtyard, lightly pushing past Leo's wide shoulders, resisting the urge to bury her face in his broad chest. She would not look at him. She could not. To do so would break her. The sun had risen while she was hiding in the alley and the bright light hit her eyes like a smack to the face. She blinked rapidly, pasting a smile onto her face. 'I am Lady Arianwen.'

All eyes turned to her and then a be-whiskered older knight was leaping from his saddle and striding towards her, his smile so wide she could see all his teeth. Behind her, Leo said nothing.

Her fingers trembled on the strap of her bag and she tightened her grip.

'Well met, Lady Arianwen. May I say, on behalf of Lord Cradoc's entire household, how pleased we are to welcome you.'

She nodded, keeping her smile in place even as her heart crumbled. She could not have spoken for the king himself, which was just as well as speech did not seem to be expected of her.

'Lord Cradoc is very anxious for your safe arrival and so I would like to begin the return journey. Where are your bags? I will send Jenkins to fetch them for you.' She must have given Jenkins directions to her room because a young man was moving towards the inn at a rapid pace. 'And is this the knight who has been escorting you?' The man was nodding towards Leo and again she must have made a sound, because the man was pulling coins out of a purse he had strapped tight to his belt and was handing them to Leo and congratulating him on a job well done and still, Leo was saying nothing.

And then she was being gently pushed towards a portly mare who looked as if anything faster than a trot would make her keel over. 'Oh, but I have my own horse,' she protested when it became clear she was supposed to ride the mottled grey mount.

'We were given instructions that the horse on which you rode here was to be returned to Lord Owain ap Llewellyn. I'm sure the knight who escorted you here can return her.'

'But Bel is my horse,' she protested weakly. She'd been able to contemplate the idea of giving Bel up when she thought that Leo would have her. She had seen how Leo treated Bosco, how he put his horse's needs before his own whenever they arrived somewhere. The thought that Bel would return to her stepfather made her sick to her stomach. Not that Bel would be mistreated but she was returning to the place Ari thought of as a prison and somehow that made her own situation worse.

The man whom she realised had not introduced himself merely smiled at her as if she hadn't spoken. Her bags, the bags that contained nothing she wanted, were being brought down from the chamber she had shared with Leo and loaded onto a wagon that was part of the retinue. She couldn't face Leo. She knew she would break if she did and he still did not say anything. There was a strange buzzing in her ear, as if an army of bees had taken up residence there.

'This here is Grey,' said the man with the impressive facial hair, patting the unimaginatively named horse on the rump. The man laughed loudly, although there was nothing humorous in his statement. 'I am Sir Timor, Lord Cradoc's most trusted knight and also his right-hand man. There is nothing the lord does that I do not know about.' Delivered with that ever-present smile, his words still caused a shiver to run down Ari's spine. Maybe it was the thought of being trapped with a man she did not know or the end of all her dreams, but the way his lips twisted upwards looked sinister. 'I believe all your bags have been collected. It is time we were on our way.'

Sir Timor offered his arm to help her onto Grey but Ari shook her head. 'One moment.' It was not a good idea for her to say her farewells to Leo. She did not want him to see her cry, did not want anyone to witness that weakness, but she found she could not climb onto the horse without speaking to him one last time.

She turned. He was standing where she had passed him, at the entrance to the alleyway. He may as well have been carved from stone for all he had moved since she had stepped into the courtyard. His expression was inscrutable, the set of his shoulders neither tense nor relaxed.

She walked over to him quickly and lightly touched his forearm. He didn't move, showing no sign that he could even see her. His jaw was clenched so tight it looked as if it hurt. She took in a shuddery breath. There was so much she wanted to say but not in front of all these strangers.

She wished she had stayed in the chamber so they would have had a few moments in private to say what needed to be said. The words she said now would have to do. 'I wish you well, Sir Leopold. I hope your life is everything you dreamed it would be. Give my regards to Tristan and Hugh and I hope that one day you and I will meet again so that you can share stories of your adventures with me.'

His lips parted as if he was about to speak but no words came out. She squeezed his arm and lightly shook her head before turning away and letting Sir Timor help her onto Grey. The men began to move slowly, Grey plodding on behind without any encouragement from her. She blinked to stop the tears from falling, concentrating on her breathing and not the fact that she was leaving behind not just Leo but also the life she had wanted for herself.

She could do this.

This was not the end of her, just the end of her dreams.

Chapter Eighteen

L eo wasn't aware of time passing. He stood staring in the direction Ari had disappeared as if she might suddenly reappear. She'd gone and he couldn't understand it, couldn't even begin to make sense of the events that had led to her leaving him. If she'd run, taken her things and disappeared into the forest, he might have been able to understand it more. But this? This was incomprehensible. After struggling for her freedom for so long, in the end she had gone willingly. It was so opposite everything he thought he'd known about Arianwen de Monfort, it would be laughable if it wasn't so tragic. She had spoken to that odd-looking stranger and smiled and acted as if the world were not ending. And Leo had stood there and let it all happen.

Eventually, he became aware of people staring at him, muttering conversations in his periphery as they clearly wondered whether he had lost his wits. Slowly, he loosened his stance, turning away from the space where Ari no longer stood and letting himself back inside the inn. The owner was watching him, obviously concerned that his guest was going to cause trouble after his unusual behaviour. Leo ignored him and trudged up the stairs until he reached the chamber he had shared with Ari.

She was still there in the scent of lavender soap and the crumpled bedsheet, suggesting she had left the chamber only a short moment ago. He blinked and he could see her before him, her legs relaxed and loose, her breasts bare to him and her smile so wide and beautiful. The look in her eyes…he could have sworn it was love or something so close that if only he'd had enough time, he could have persuaded her to love him as much as he did her. This was what hell looked like, the empty shell of what could have been.

There was nothing in this place that belonged to him. His saddlebags were still attached to Bosco. He would collect his horse and Bel and be on his way. He swallowed once, twice, but it did nothing to relieve the pain in his throat. He turned and left the chamber.

Bel knickered softly at his approach and he rubbed the mare's nose. 'She's not here.' And although he knew that Bel could not understand his words, he could have sworn that sadness filled the horse's eyes.

He didn't remember saddling up Bosco or leaving the stables, or travelling through the streets of the town, but somehow he found himself out in the open and he glanced at the road that led towards Pembroke. There was no sign of Ari and her entourage. She was truly gone. He would never see her again, never hear the laughter in her voice as she teased him, never pit his wits against hers, never watch the way her supple body moved.

He turned the horses towards the route that would take him back to Abertawe, where he could deliver Bel and then travel on to St David's and Tristan. His mission was accomplished, he had succeeded in delivering Lady Arianwen, but whenever he'd pictured this moment before, he'd been triumphant. Why, then, did he want to howl in despair, to tear the world to pieces and to ride hard and fast in the opposite direction?

Because Ari had sacrificed her own dreams for him, that was why. She'd had the perfect moment to slip away. She'd heard him deny he knew of her whereabouts; she must have done because she had been right behind him. She could have got away, could have run just like she'd always planned, and he would have done nothing to stop her, would have pretended to search for her and thrown the party off any trace of her he might have found. He hadn't had time to think about all the implications but he'd known in that moment that whatever the consequences, he would have faced them for her.

Instead, she had walked towards her destiny with her head held high. It was not his right to be proud of her but he was. The way she had comported herself, as if she were the queen, striding amongst those men as if she wanted to go with them and they were there to suit her demands, not the other way around. If he hadn't known otherwise, he would have thought she welcomed her new future. She'd been magnificent, her bravery outstripping anyone he'd ever met.

He pulled the horses to a stop in the middle of the path. This was wrong. Very, very wrong. There was no way that his being apart from Ari could ever be considered the right thing. He should never have accepted her sacrifice without saying something to her. Anything would have been better than the unending silence he had given her as the events had unfolded. He'd always thought himself a brave man, but in that moment, when it counted, he had been a coward and had lost the most important battle of his life.

Somehow, over the course of the journey, Ari's happiness had become more important to him than anything else. More important than proving his worth to his parents or becoming a warrior of renown. He'd been chasing the wrong thing all this time. Ari had tried to tell him but he hadn't been ready to listen. In not rescuing Ari and allowing her to go free, he had let her down and that lacerated him far more than disappointing his parents ever would. He now knew he would sacrifice anything for her but he was coming to that realisation too late. Instead of trusting his instincts, he had tried to be more methodical to follow the rules, and in doing so, he had made the worst mistake of his life.

There was something off about Sir Timor too, and if Leo hadn't been so wrapped up in his own selfish grief, he would have questioned the man more. Hell, he hadn't even checked that these men did belong to Lord Cradoc. So much for being a chivalrous knight! Right at this moment, he wasn't even worthy to call himself a man.

In front of him lay the path towards Abertawe. He could follow it; he *should* follow it. He owed it to Tristan and Hugh to come to their aid as soon as possible. He had promised them that he would; he had promised Ari that he would see her delivered to her betrothed and nothing more. Had told her repeatedly that he would ensure that she reached Lord Cradoc. He had done everything he had said he would and he should be proud of a mission successfully completed. And yet… And yet his heart was splintering into a thousand pieces. Ari's bravery eclipsed his a hundredfold. She was the one worthy of becoming a celebrated knight and Leo was not, especially if he allowed this travesty to happen. She had as much right to shape her own future as any man.

He whirled Bosco round. It was time to act.

Chapter Nineteen

'Lord Cradoc will see you now,' Sir Timor told Ari as he held open a large wooden door.

Ari pulled her cloak tighter around herself. She had been left to wait in this antechamber since she had arrived at Lord Cradoc's stronghold some time ago. The fire wasn't lit and although it was summer, it was bitterly cold this deep within the castle walls. But none of that was why she was shaking. Being left alone for so long had stripped her of her confidence. It had left her questioning herself and her place within this household. She tried to hold on to her father's voice. He'd taught her that messing with your opponent's mind was just as important as attacking them with a weapon. This arrangement wasn't meant to be a war. It was supposed to be a marriage, a new start for both her and her betrothed, but being kept waiting like this did not seem like the actions of a man desperate to take a wife. This was a move a person would make if they wanted to assert their dominance. She'd been subjected to her stepfather's machinations enough times to recognise the tactic. She did not like that Lord Cradoc was already winning but she would not show it. She would not show that she had been affected in any way by her prolonged stay in this unwelcoming chamber.

She nodded briefly to Lord Cradoc's right-hand man. He had been relentlessly cheerful on the short ride to this castle. At first, she had been grateful for his endless chatter because it had stopped her thinking about everything she had given up and the man she had left behind. After a while his chatter had begun to feel forced and she had attempted to join in. Every time she'd tried to ask a question, he'd deflected until she had eventually stopped trying.

Sir Timor held the thick wooden door open and gestured for her to hurry up and enter. It seemed he was not leaving her to greet her betrothed alone. She passed the knight and entered a small chamber. A fire roared ferociously in a fireplace that took up most of one wall, Ari resisted the urge to run to it and warm her hands. Instead, she moved into the middle of the chamber, her hands clasped in front of her in that demure way she knew her stepfather liked so much. Lord Cradoc, withered and grey-haired, stood and walked towards her. He circled her, not speaking as he completed his inspection. A shiver ran down her spine but she held herself still. She would show no weakness in front of this man.

'She's lost weight since I last saw her. She must eat more if she is to be strong enough to carry my heir.' Heat burned her skin as Lord Cradoc discussed her body as if she were not there.

'Yes, my lord.'

'What happened to her hair?'

'That I do not know.'

Ari dug her fingernails into the palms of her hands. It did not matter that he was not talking to her. Nothing mattered.

Lord Cradoc grunted. 'It will grow back, I suppose. Make sure she does not cut it short again.'

'Of course.'

'Have you told her what I expect from her?' asked Lord Cradoc, still addressing Sir Timor.

'I thought you would like to tell her yourself. She will better understand the gravity if the words come directly from you.'

'Perhaps you are right.' Lord Cradoc turned to her, his icy blue eyes boring into her soul. 'You are to be my wife and I expect your behaviour to reflect that. You will only speak when addressed, you will devote your life to quiet reflection, you will never speak against me, either to my face or to anyone in the castle and you will provide me with heirs.' Ari said nothing. 'We are to be married on Friday.' She still said nothing. Friday was two days away. Two days until she tied herself to this man who had yet to offer her a kind word, or any word that was not an order. She had made her choice and she would abide by it but she knew now for certain that it would come at the cost of her soul. 'Sir Timor, escort Lady Arianwen to her chamber.'

Lord Cradoc didn't acknowledge her as she left his chamber.

'He is very set in his ways,' said Sir Timor, his jovial tone grating against Ari's skin as they wound their way through narrow, barely lit corridors, 'but you will come to understand him soon enough and when there are heirs on the way…well, I am sure we will all be happy.'

Ari licked her lips. They felt dry beneath her touch. 'We?'

Surprisingly, Sir Timor answered her. 'Lord Cradoc has not been himself since his first wife and their children passed away. He will be content once more when we have a couple of heirs for this place and that will benefit us all.'

Ari closed her eyes briefly. A couple of heirs! She did not know if she could bear to lie with the man once. If he could not dredge up comforting words when first meeting the woman who was to be his wife, then it was hardly likely he would treat her with any courtesy in the bedchamber. He would not learn the ways to make her body sing or treat her body like it was something to be revered, not like Leo had.

'Here is the chamber you will stay in until your marriage.' Sir Timor held open another door, nowhere near as ornate as the last one, and gestured for her to enter. 'I will see about someone bringing you a candle,' he murmured as he peered inside. There was no light coming from the room, no suggestion that there was a window with shutters or anything that let natural light in. Sir Timor was still holding the door open and she had no choice but to step inside. 'Someone will be along with a candle shortly,' he told her before pulling the door shut, leaving her all alone.

She whirled around as she was plunged into absolute darkness, her heart hammering in her throat. Then came the unmistakable sound of a key turning in the lock and everything inside her stilled.

She'd been locked into her chamber like a prisoner.

She blinked slowly, her eyes trying to adjust to the darkness, her mind almost unable to comprehend the depths of her captivity. She didn't know how long she stood there but finally rage flooded through her, thick and molten. How dare they treat her with such disrespect? As if she were nothing but a vessel for producing heirs, as if it did not matter that she was in a strange place alone and in the dark.

Well, if either man thought this treatment would break her, they were very, very wrong. True, she had never been incarcerated at the behest of her stepfather, but he had tried other ways to destroy her spirit and she had prevailed. She would do so again. She took a deep breath to steady her resolve. She might be in darkness but she could still explore her surroundings. She held out her hand, moving towards where she had last seen the door. From there she moved to her left. Her fingers found thick tapestries hanging on a wall, so this chamber was probably decent if only she could see in it. She moved around the space, keeping one hand on the fabric as she made her way around. In this fashion she discovered a bare table and a bed with luxurious coverings. She crawled on top of them. She'd not found any of her belongings, not even her small bag with her only true possessions. Her stomach writhed at the thought of what was happening to them. There was nothing she could do about it right now. She had barely slept the night before and so far the day had been mentally and physically draining, so she closed her eyes and let herself sleep.

She awoke to the delivery of a candle and the news that she was to be escorted to the Great Hall for the evening repast. She'd been left in the dark for some time then, she gathered. It was as well that she had used the time wisely by getting some much-needed rest instead of panicking. Holding her head high, she followed the servant back through the long corridors and into the Great Hall. She was seated beside Lord Cradoc and found it was very easy to follow his decree not to speak to him until she was spoken to. There was no one with whom she wanted to converse. Lord Cradoc's bony fingers picked at the food in front of him, his gimlet gaze intent on the people who ate before him. Despite the dour expression of their lord, Ari was surprised to find the atmosphere quite jovial. Conversation soon floated up to her and she realised that her appearance at the high table was the reason for the good mood.

'…now he's got a pretty wife…'

'…so much younger than him…'

'Can you imagine lying beneath him?'

'It would be like swiving a skeleton.'

There was laughter at this. Ari's hands tightened on her spoon but Lord Cradoc showed no reaction as salacious commentary carried on around them.

'Some babes will…'

'…so sour since his wife died that…'

Ari glanced down at her food. She was hungry and the meal was tasty but she could not bring herself to force down another bite. It was slowly dawning on her why people were so pleased to see her. They wanted her to change their lord and master into someone who smiled. It was possible of course that she might be able to do it but at what cost to her soul?

Sensing that she would not be permitted to leave the

Hall until Lord Cradoc was ready, she sat with her hands folded in her lap, her body as still as possible. Still, that is, until a flash of something caught her eye. She watched as one of the young squires tossed a dagger into the air, twirling it round for everyone to see. Without even thinking she was on her feet and striding towards him. She caught the blade midair, the metal handle smacking against the palm of her hand. 'That's mine.'

The young man stared at her, his mouth agape.

'Lady Arianwen! What do you think you are doing?'

For a frail-looking man, Lord Cradoc had followed her over to the corner of the room with surprising speed. She brandished the dagger she was holding. 'This was my father's. He gave it to me. This man is playing with something that does not belong to him.'

The silence in the Hall was thick. The veins in Lord Cradoc's neck bulged. 'Everything you brought with you now belongs to me. I chose to give this squire that blade because of his performance today. You will return the dagger to him and you will not question my decision.'

She gripped the handle tighter. She would make many sacrifices but not this. 'No.'

Lord Cradoc's lips were so thin she could no longer see them. 'Your stepfather warned me of your disobedience but I did not think you would need to be disciplined so soon. Men, take Lady Arianwen to her chamber. She will remain there until our wedding. Hopefully, she will have learned her lesson by then.'

Ari dodged the first man who lunged for her and rammed her fist into the second but they kept coming and soon she was overwhelmed. She struggled all the way through the corridors but her captors held her tight.

Later, she would be proud that it took four men to subdue her but right now, she was only furious.

By the time she reached her chamber she was burning with anger and shame. Somebody opened the door and she was shoved inside before the door was slammed shut behind her and the key turned ominously in the lock. Someone had snuffed out the candle and she was left in darkness once more. Fury had her spinning around and pounding on the wooden door, yelling words of anger and frustration, but nobody responded to her and she slumped against it, exhausted and destroyed.

'Making friends, I see,' said a voice from the far corner of the chamber.

She screamed, whirling round, hands raised to face her invisible intruder.

'Calm down. It's only me.'

'Leo!' she hissed, her heart pounding so hard she thought it might burst.

'Shush. We don't want the whole town to be alerted to my presence.'

'What are you doing in here? You need to leave. You need…' Her words trailed off and she realised that tears were rolling unheeded down her cheeks. She wiped them away but they continued to fall.

'Hey.' She heard him take a few steps towards her. 'Where are you?'

She held out a hand. His body brushed against hers and then he was pulling her into his arms and she was sobbing, crying harder than she ever had, into his solid chest. He held her tightly, not saying anything as she wept against him, distress mixing with fury. He held her until the storm had passed and she fell against him, completely spent.

'You're here,' she whispered.

'Yes.'

'Why?'

'To get you out.'

'What?' She lifted her head to look at him but she could barely even make out the shape of him in the darkness.

He cleared his throat. 'It occurred to me that I had completed my task successfully. I have witnesses who saw me hand you over and coins as my token of appreciation from Lord Cradoc, which I can show to Sir Benedictus to prove that I am a capable, competent, honourable knight. I have done my part and I can hold my head up high when I meet up with my brother knights.'

She frowned. She knew he had completed his mission. Her sacrifice had allowed him to do so, but coming here to boast to her about it was both out of character and dangerous.

'But,' he continued, 'nobody gave me instructions as to what was to happen after I delivered you to Lord Cradoc.'

'I don't follow.'

'I've come to get you out of here.'

Her fingers flexed against his arms. 'If you remove me from here, that will void the successful completion of your mission.' She did not dare to hope that what he suggested might be possible. It was too hard to hope for freedom only to have it taken away from her again; it would be more than she could bear right now.

'If nobody finds out I'm responsible for your disappearance then…' She felt him shrug. 'I will be in the clear but… Ari, I could not let you sacrifice yourself for me. To know that you had given up your freedom so that I might have a chance of becoming a member of the King's Knights would be intolerable. I would not be able to live with myself as a man or become any sort of knight, let alone one who helped to defend the Kingdom, if I knowingly let you suffer for the sake of something I want. Hell, I could not be the man I want to be if I allowed that.'

Her heart twisted even as it swelled with hope. His words weren't the declaration she was hoping for. She'd thought he might be here because he loved her and didn't want to let her out of his life, but his being here for any reason was enough right now. To know that she wasn't on her own, that there was someone who would fight with her, was a miracle she had never expected. But if it was because of a sense of duty, not love, she should not hold on to him any longer, should not kiss him again, because it would be too painful. She pulled herself from his arms and heard his hands drop to his sides.

For now, she needed to focus on the practicalities. Everything else could come later. Leo might have made it into her chamber but getting out was another matter. 'How did you know where my chamber was? How did you get into it and how will we get out now that they have locked the door?'

He huffed out a laugh. 'As if I would come to you without a clear plan. Getting out of the chamber is easy. I'm surprised you do not know how to pick locks, but I am pleased to be able to do one thing better than you.'

'You are able to do a lot of things better than me,' she said truthfully.

'Hmm, a compliment. You must be feeling out of sorts.'

She smiled her first genuinely happy smile since she had last seen him. 'Don't let it add to your arrogance.'

He laughed again. 'Don't worry. I'm quite sure that when I teach you how to pick a lock, you will surpass me within days of learning the new skill.'

She was surprised to feel tears welling in her eyes once more. She was not normally this emotional and she certainly didn't cry over praise. She was glad of the darkness so that he could not see her reaction, but he seemed to know anyway as he reached up and brushed them away with the pad of his thumb, his touch sweeping across her cheeks.

'Getting you out of the castle will be harder but not impossible, I think. This place is hardly Windsor. The guards are not expecting trouble and are mostly interested in their game of dice. Or at least they were earlier.'

'How long have you been here?'

'Roughly the same length of time as you.'

'What? How?'

'It did not take me long to catch up with you and your entourage. You were exceptionally slow. It was the work of a moment to slip inside the castle walls. As I said, nobody seems to be expecting an attack. We will slip out together and with luck they will not notice you are missing until tomorrow morning. By then, we will be long gone.'

Neither of them commented that it could be even longer before anyone noticed she was missing. It could be some time before anyone came looking for her.

'What was that noise when you first came into the chamber?' asked Leo.

'What noise?' She'd been so furious she hadn't heard anything other than the thundering of her heart.

'There was a distinct thud as if something heavy was hitting the ground.'

'My dagger!' she exclaimed, dropping to the floor and feeling around on the flagstones. 'Lord Cradoc took it and gave it to a page without telling me. I took it back, which infuriated him, and in the commotion nobody noticed I still held on to it.' Her fingers closed around the cool metal of the handle. 'I've got it.' She ran her fingers along the familiar design, the loops and whorls that she knew better than her own hand soothing her. Nobody would take this from her again, not without a fight.

She pushed herself to her feet. She had a way to get out of here and a blade with which to defend herself. She was as ready as she ever would be to escape. 'Let's go.'

'There's no rush.'

'There is plenty of rush.'

He laughed softly. 'I don't think that statement makes sense but even if it did I would urge you to be cautious. We want the castle to have quietened down for the night and that may take longer than normal after the drama at the feast. People will want to discuss what happened to you and what it might mean for your marriage.'

He had a point. 'That sounds sensible.'

He whistled quietly. 'That's two compliments now. I don't think I'll be able to stop them going to my head after all.'

She laughed. The release was so wonderful that she found she couldn't stop. Soon she was clutching at her sides, tears of mirth streaming down her face.

'I'm sorry,' she managed when she was finally able

to get herself under control. 'I don't know what's wrong with me.'

After a brief pause, he said, 'There's nothing wrong with you. You are perfect.' Before she could respond, he added, 'It's that bastard, Lord Cradoc, who's the problem.'

She sobered. 'Have you found out any more about him since you and I were last together?'

'No. But a man who shuts his bride up in a dark room deserves no place in this world.'

'I think he has become sad since the death of his wife and children. Perhaps that's what drives his actions.'

'All the more reason to treat you with compassion.'

'Grief does strange things to a person.'

'It does but that still does not excuse his behaviour. You lost your father at a young age and yet you are still a good person.'

'I think my father's death has shaped me, though, perhaps in ways it would not have done had he lived. I am ashamed to say that I have been angry with him.' The darkness made it easier to confess her shameful thoughts.

'You have? You always speak of him with such pride.'

She swallowed. 'I started to think he had lied to me— or perhaps to himself. I felt let down by him but now I think he truly believed I would become a warrior. I think you see me as a worthy opponent.'

'I do.' His response was instant and unequivocal. She believed that he meant it. He was not telling her what she wanted to hear in order to get her to do something. He truly did believe in her.

'Your faith in me has reminded me that not all men are like my stepfather. Some can believe it is possible for women to be as capable on the battlefield as men. My father was like you. I had forgotten but now I remember and it fills me with a happiness that neither Lord Owain or Lord Cradoc can take away.'

'I am glad. You deserve to be happy.'

'As do you.' It would not be easy to say her next words. Hell, she did not want to say them at all but now that she was calmer, she knew what she must do. 'I know that you have come to rescue me from marriage to a man who will make me miserable and you will never know how much that means to me, but I cannot allow you to sacrifice yourself. You must leave before anyone sees you here and you must go without me.'

He grunted. 'No, Ari. I will do neither of these things.'

'But what about your family? If they find out that you went against the orders of your lord and stole me away then you will not gain their respect, the exact opposite, in fact.' Ari did not want Leo to resent her for the choice he had made. She had accepted her fate and was resigned to it. 'I thought that was what you wanted above all things. I do not want to take that away from you.'

'Now is not the time to argue with me, Ari.'

'I'm serious, Leo.' She tugged at his sleeve. 'If we get caught or if there is any hint you were involved in my escape, the life you have wanted for as long as you can remember will be over. You need to think clearly about this.'

He sighed, although the sound was laced with something else—fondness and a hint of amusement. 'I would not be here if I had not thought clearly about this. I know myself to be impulsive but in this I am sure of my direction. Being with you has made me think seriously about my own desires. Lord Owain sought to make you into someone you are not and yet you kept your faith, even when it seemed impossible, that you were meant to be a warrior. You did not allow his opinion of you to change who you are. This is how I will live my live from now on. I am who I am. You were right about my family. Their opinion of me must not be allowed to shape my actions going forward. I am in charge of how I feel about myself, and if I conduct myself with honour then that is what matters. Making sure you can lead the life you want to, *that* will make *me* proud of my actions.'

He paused while she absorbed this, her heart fluttering with hope.

'We are going to leave this chamber together,' he continued. 'And we are going to get you out of the castle and free you from Lord Cradoc's soul-destroying presence. If I can avoid being seen by anyone within the castle, then all the better. But if I am and word gets back to Lord Ormand or Sir Benedictus, well, your freedom will be worth it. You were…'

He paused and she wished she could see his expression. He cleared his throat and she smiled. She'd noticed he had a habit of doing that when he had something serious to say.

'You were willing to sacrifice your freedom for me. It is only fair that I risk the same.'

Her heart swelled, seeming to expand in her chest to an almost painful degree. Nobody had ever put her first, not even her father. Ari knew her father had loved her, but he had loved her mother more. She had always been second place her whole life, until now. Leo was giving her more than her freedom; he was giving her his trust and faith and that meant more to her than anything.

'You should get some rest,' said Leo, the serious moment passing without a comment from her.

'I've had lots. All I did this afternoon was sleep.'

'Still, we will need all our wits about us if we are to get out of here without detection. We have no idea how long that will take. We may need to fight our way out and, after that, we will likely be riding all night. At least sit down and try to rest.'

She huffed out a breath and moved in the direction of the bed. 'You should join me.'

There was a pause. 'I don't think that's a good idea. I need to stay focused and alert.'

As Ari settled onto the straw mattress, she didn't ask him to elaborate. She knew full well to what he was referring and although she could see sense in his decision, it didn't stop a wave of disappointment. They lapsed into silence. She traced the markings on her dagger handle with her thumb, the images conjuring up images of her father. Would he be proud of the decisions that had led her to this point in her life? She knew he would have liked Leo. He'd be impressed by his skills and his focus, and her father would admire his actions today. Would he think Leo worthy of her love? She would never know and a familiar ache settled in her chest, the ache that reminded her that she would never speak to her father again, would never hear his deep laugh or bask in his proud gaze. This time the ache was tempered with something else: gratitude that she had had such good times with him, that he had been there to shower her with praise about her fighting skills and to give her unconditional support. She had never doubted, for a moment, that he loved her. Even though she and her mother had not understood one another, she knew her mother loved her and wanted the best for her too.

She'd never thought she would fall in love. Never thought she would meet a man who inspired feelings like the ones she had for Leo. She wasn't sure if he felt the same way. He very obviously enjoyed the time they had spent in bed together. He respected her and enjoyed her company, and he had come here to rescue her, but...he had stressed that he was here to save her because it was the right thing to do. He had not said that the thought of her being married to someone else was sending him out of his mind or that he cared for her more than as a friend. He had spoken often of a future that did not have room in it for a wife or a woman. Besides, she was not cut out to be someone's spouse. She would not be content with sitting around embroidering, waiting for Leo to come back from battle. It would break her to hear his stories, to hear tales of his adventures, and not to have participated in them as well. No, she loved him but there was no future for them and she would not make their last moments together awkward by expressing feelings that might not be reciprocated.

She was so lost in her thoughts that she didn't notice the time passing until she heard Leo's footsteps on the flagstones moving away from her. She straightened as he came to a stop and then there was a strange scratching sound.

'What's that noise?' she whispered.

'I'm picking the lock,' he responded quietly.

'Is it difficult?'

'It's as easy as getting you tipsy on sweetened ale.'

She gasped. 'I knew that was what you were trying to do.'

'And yet you still continued to drink it.'

'It was delicious. Besides, I didn't tell you anything.'

'No, you didn't. I will have to try a different technique next time.'

He laughed, his seriousness from earlier replaced by his normal easy-going good humour. Then the door was creaking open slowly, a soft beam of light hitting the floor and throwing Leo into shadow. He held still for a moment, staring out into the long corridor, and then gestured for her to join him.

He jumped when she touched his arm. 'I apologise. I didn't mean to scare you.'

He snorted. 'I wasn't scared. I didn't realise you were so close, that's all. You move silently.'

'That's good to know for our current situation.'

He started to move but she caught his sleeve. 'How did you find me in the woods that day?'

'Why do you want to know that now?' He sounded incredulous.

'It seems like a good idea to know what gave me away, so I don't make the same mistake now.'

He inhaled as if he was about to speak but then nothing…

'What is it?'

'It was Bel.'

'Bel?'

'Yes. I thought I heard the softest of whinnies and I charged through the woods looking for you. I'll admit

I was frantic by that stage. Finding you was luck not a mistake on your part.'

Ari nodded, a chill creeping down her back. Leo was good at tracking her despite what he thought but there were so many things to think about in this escape and there was no time to plan. There was no doubt in her mind that she and Leo were skilled fighters, but this was a castle full of people. It would not take many men to overwhelm them.

Leo made to step out of the chamber, but she grabbed his arm, stopping him in his tracks. 'What if we're caught?'

'We won't be.' Leo sounded confident but she could hear the faint trace of doubt in his voice.

'We might be, and if we are...' She swallowed. 'It will be awful.'

She heard his long exhale and then he said simply, 'Yes, it will.'

'They'll probably kill you.' Before, with the door closed, Ari had thought only of how their discovery would result in Leo not becoming the knight he wanted to be, but now, just as they were about to embark on the most dangerous part of the escape, she realised that the consequences would be far more serious. Leo would be accused of abducting Lord Cradoc's bride. He would hang.

She tightened her grip on his arm. 'I cannot let you do this. You must leave without me.'

The thought of the world without Leo in it was too much to contemplate. She would rather be married to Lord Cradoc for all of eternity than face that reality.

He covered her hand with one of his own. 'Ari, I

know you're scared but trust me, this will work and, if it doesn't, it will be worth the risk.'

'I'm not frightened for me. I just don't want you to get hurt. I cannot live with your death on my conscience. You must—'

But before she could finish her sentence, he was pulling her from the chamber and softly closing her door behind him. The light in the corridor was only marginally better than the room but at least she could see his face now.

'Leo,' she hissed, but he ignored her as he bent over to fiddle with the lock. 'Leo, I mean it. You must put me back in the chamber and leave.'

He straightened. 'No. We've been through this already. We are leaving together. For once, do not argue with me.'

'But—'

He covered her mouth with his hand. 'Arianwen de Monfort, we are leaving this castle together. Every moment you argue this with me, we waste time. I didn't take you for a coward.' Even though she knew he was trying to annoy her in order to get her moving, his insult still worked. She straightened her spine and he dropped his hand, his eyes dancing with amusement.

'Fine, we're going, but if you get yourself killed, don't come complaining to me.'

'Oh, I will. I will haunt you every moment of every day for the rest of your time on earth.'

And with that they were off, whispering light insults at each other as they made their way down the long corridor, knowing that they didn't mean them but that their conversation was a good way to keep the fear from paralysing them both.

They came to a stop just before the corridor took a sharp turn to the left. The light had been getting stronger as they had made their way along, and Ari guessed they were coming close to the burning lanterns that lit the passageways near the Great Hall.

They waited, listening for any sound to suggest that there was anyone around the corner. Only the noise of their breathing filled the air. Leo took a step forward and froze, Ari bumping into him with a soft thud. He pushed against her, backing them both up against the wall as voices carried to them.

'Hell of a way to start the union,' a man laughed.

'I always said it was a bad idea, him wedding a beautiful young woman,' another man responded. 'Should have picked a widow, like himself. Someone with a few babes already. Someone less spirited.'

'Aye, they're going to be miserable together, I have no doubt. She's too much of a wild cat for our miserly lord, but at least it was an entertaining evening. I haven't seen that much action in the Great Hall in years, if ever.'

The voices were getting louder, at least two of them, moving slowly, gossiping about this evening's events. There was nowhere else for the two men to go except towards Leo and Ari, unless they turned around. Once they were past this corner, the men would find the fugitives backed against this wall and then who knew what would happen. Ari tightened her grip on her dagger, the handle slippery in her palm. In front of her, Leo's hand went slowly to the hilt of his sword; he loosened it in its scabbard and Ari closed her eyes. It was one thing to fight men in battle or in self-defence, but quite another to take the lives of two people because they were in the wrong place at the wrong time.

'Can't say I blame her for losing her temper, though. Imagine that old bastard taking all you have left and giving it to a page!'

'Oh, aye. Can't blame her at all. Anyone would feel the same.'

Ari's stomach twisted as she listened. The two men were offering her words of support, even though, as far as they were concerned, she would never know of their support. From the tightening of Leo's shoulders, he was thinking along the same lines. She and Leo could not end the lives of these two men just because it suited their purposes. It was too high a price to pay for freedom.

Leo held himself as still as possible. Part of his mind was calculating the width of the corridor, working out the best way to take down the two men walking towards them. The other part of him was wondering whether he could really do it, destroy two men who'd done nothing wrong except get in the way of his escape. Because there really was no way they could avoid each other. This corridor only went one way.

Behind him, pressed against his back, Ari's whole body was trembling. He knew she wasn't afraid for herself—she was fearless—but she would not like taking the lives of the two men coming towards them, not when their death was weighed against her freedom. Sure enough, she tugged on his sleeve. 'I can't,' she whispered into the shell of his ear. 'We have to go back.'

It was too late for that. The two men would see them moving. There was a small chance they would not spot

Ari in front of his bulk and would think he was a member of the castle moving about like themselves, but he could not take the risk.

He pulled his sword from his scabbard.

'Leo,' she said urgently. 'They are innocent men.'

Leo did not soften his stance but he heard what she was saying and agreed. 'We'll lock them in the chamber,' he murmured. It was a compromise. It meant the men would live but not be able to sound an alarm immediately. They would be found eventually and the search party would be wide and far. It would become known that Leo had been involved in Ari's escape, and he could say goodbye to the King's Knights, and to Tristan and Hugh too. He had to hope that they would forgive him someday. Better that than the deaths of two defenceless men on his conscience.

He waited. Ari's body continued to shake and he wanted to turn and pull her into his arms to comfort her and convince her that everything would work out, but he could make no such promises when he didn't know himself.

He waited, but the corridor had fallen silent.

They waited some more. Behind him, some of the tension left Ari's body. 'Perhaps they've gone,' she whispered. Her breath caressed the nape of his neck and he shivered; funny how he could have that reaction to her now when there was so much at stake.

He shook his head. 'We would have heard their footsteps retreating. They're still there.'

'What are they doing?'

A soft grunt gave Leo a fairly good idea what was going on. He waited. Another grunt was followed by a soft moan and it had him mostly convinced. To be sure, he peered around the corner, pulling back quickly, although he doubted either man would spot him at this moment.

'What is it?'

'See for yourself.'

She leaned around him.

'Oh.'

The tension in her body left in a whoosh and she collapsed against him. His arm came up, caging her, holding her tight, his own arms trembling with relief or some other emotion.

'I don't think they're going anywhere soon,' she said against his chest.

'No,' agreed Leo.

'We'll wait for them to finish and then they'll probably head back to wherever they came from. We won't have to hurt them at all.' Ari sounded delighted but Leo was having a very different reaction. The noises were getting louder and more obvious and Ari was now pressed against his front, her scent filling his nostrils. Reason was slowly draining from his mind to be replaced by an all-encompassing desire. He wanted to push her away, to stop this loss of control before it swamped him entirely, but he also wanted to lift her skirts and plunge into her mindlessly. He knew he could do neither and the restraint was a new kind of torture.

The wait for it to be over seemed endless. At some point, Ari picked up on his desire and her own breathing became rapid. She shifted restlessly against him and his arm tensed around her, holding her in place. If she moved again, he would be lost.

With a final groan, the noises stopped. The two men started muttering in low voices to one another, but Leo could not hear what was being said. Eventually, footsteps sounded up again but this time they were moving away from their hiding spot. Leo loosened his grip and moved away from Ari.

'That was…interesting,' she said.

Leo nodded, finding he could not look at her. Despite exploring her with his lips and tongue, and knowing how she sounded as he pleasured her, he was embarrassed by his reaction to what had passed. The noise of two lovers and her body against his had nearly sent him out of his mind. All those years of training had not prepared him for that. Perhaps Lord Ormand was right and he was not fit—

'You're doing it again.'

He looked across at her. Her arms were folded as she leaned back against the opposite wall. 'What am I doing?'

'You're being your own worst enemy. You're telling yourself you're not worthy.'

He raised his eyebrows, trying to adopt the air of someone who had not been thinking that exact thing.

'Is it because you didn't charge around the corner and take those two men, or is it because you got a bit—' her eyes flashed to his groin and back to his face '—you know…' She raised a suggestive eyebrow.

Heat rushed across his face, hotter than the sun. 'I…'

'Because instead of listening to your self-doubts, you should listen to me. You showed good judgement. Instead of death, those two men got to spend some, by the sounds of it, very enjoyable private time together. As for your reaction, well…' And now her cheeks were turning pink, 'I was similarly affected.'

He grinned, the tension draining out of him. She was exactly right. He had been talking himself down when there was no need. He did not need to battle with his own thoughts as well as try to get them both out of here. It would only make it harder. Instead, he should concentrate on the positives. They hadn't made it out of the castle yet but they were out of her chamber and they had not yet got into a fight. As for his body's reaction, well, it was not something he had ever had to deal with before, but now he knew he could hold his head together even when his body was clamouring for him to do other things. Not that he would be in that scenario again. Once Ari was free, what would she do? She would not trade her desire to become a warrior to be a good little wife to him. She knew what she wanted and he loved her enough to let her go.

He stepped forward, leaning around the corner. The corridor was empty and he signalled for her to follow him. They ghosted down the length of it, moving quickly but quietly.

They were getting close to the Great Hall now. He could hear the muted voices of several conversations but they were no longer those of people eating. It sounded like the inhabitants, those who slept in the Great Hall, were settling down for the night. Perhaps they were gossiping more because of the events of the evening, or perhaps this was normal. The noise was a good thing as it would muffle their footsteps but it also increased the likelihood of being discovered. One more corner and they would be there.

He stopped and once more Ari ploughed into the back of him. 'You should warn me when you are going to do that,' she muttered.

'We're at the Great Hall,' he told her. 'If I stop abruptly again, it's because I'm dead.'

'Don't joke about that sort of thing.'

He didn't respond that he wasn't joking. From here on in they could not retreat. They had to keep going forward, whatever happened.

'On the other side of the entrance to the Hall there is a small door for servants to go in and out,' he said. 'Once we turn the corner, we must race to it. I don't know if the doors to the Hall will be open or closed. From the rumble of voices, I suspect ajar but I cannot be sure.'

'How can you be so sure this servants' door will be unbarred?'

He was not sure, there was no certainty in any of this, but saying this out loud would only add panic to the situation. Far better to hope for the best. 'This is a servants' passage and servants need access day and night. Pages stay up all night to ensure the fires keep burning and that the soldiers on watch receive food and drink. Trust me, I've been one of those boys. No one will question the opening and closing of a door because they will assume it is part of the regular routine.' At least that was what he hoped. Nothing could really prepare them for this. They just had to take a chance.

Leo peered around the corner. There was no one standing outside the Great Hall. It was now or never.

'Let's go.' Ari laced her fingers with his and even in this moment of terror he could appreciate how well they fitted together. He squeezed her fingers and she returned the pressure before they hurried towards their escape.

As they approached, Leo could see that the entrance to the Hall was slightly open but it was too late now to go back; they had to keep going. Ari slowed as she obviously realised it as well, but he didn't stop and she followed along with him. Thankfully, the servants' door was unlocked and then, they were out, breathing in the cool night air.

'We made it,' whispered Ari.

They had made it past the first difficult part, that was true, but they still had some way to go. He turned to tell her that but his words failed him. Ari was staring up at the sky, moonlight bathing her face in an ethereal glow. She was always beautiful but tonight she was otherworldly, and his heart tumbled wildly in his chest. He gazed at her, learning every angle, every ridge, so that when he could no longer see her, he would always be able to recall this image.

'What now?' she asked, turning to him.

He gave himself a mental shake. It was time for the next part of the plan. He had to stop gazing at Ari like a lovesick fool. 'Now we climb over the wall.'

She blinked. 'I'm sorry, it sounded like you said we have to go over the high fortifications designed to keep invaders out and people like us inside.'

His lips twitched. 'We can hardly ask them to raise the portcullis for us, can we?'

He waited while she absorbed his words. 'Can we wait until morning? When they send out a search party, we could slip out unseen.'

He'd considered that and already dismissed the idea. 'It's too risky.'

'Surely not as risky as falling from a great height and breaking our necks.'

'Has anyone ever told you that you're very dramatic?'

'Yes, but this time it's for a good reason. Do you even have a rope?'

Her gaze flickered over his body and he couldn't help it, even though their situation was perilous he wanted, no he *needed*, to tease her. 'What do we need rope for? We can use the natural footholds the stones provide us.' She glared at him and he laughed, smiling even wider when he saw her lips twitch as well. 'Of course I have rope. I took it from their stores earlier. This is not the first time I have done this.'

'Really? I cannot imagine a time when this exact scenario has happened to you before.'

'Not this exactly, no,' he said, guiding them around the edge of the castle walls, keeping close to the shadows they threw up. 'But I have climbed down the side of a castle using rope before on more than one occasion. I know what I'm doing.'

'Why have you climbed down castle walls before?'

'As part of my training. In the event of being captured we had to know how to escape. Or at least that's what our trainers told us. It may have been because Lord Ormand enjoyed watching the terror of the young men under his guardianship performing the task.'

'Were you ever frightened?'

He hesitated. He'd been about to tell her what he always said, that no, he'd never been afraid of heights, that from his very first go he was fine about undertaking such an ordeal, but it was not true. He knew he did not need to pretend to Ari. He knew that to confess to being frightened would not change how she saw him. It was a freeing revelation. He could be completely himself with her, in a way he had never been with anyone else. 'At first, yes, I was very afraid. I thought I would die from the fear, if not from the falling from a great height. Once I got used to it, I was still afraid. I thought I would embarrass myself in some way, be sick or cry or something. But over the years I became numb to the fear, so believe me when I tell you that I will not fail you when we do this.'

'I know you won't. You have not yet and you never will, but I want you to know that it's normal to be afraid. I would think you inhuman if you weren't.'

His heart swelled. He had revealed a part of himself that he had kept hidden and she still had faith in him. He brought them to a stop beside stairs, which led up to the ramparts. He dropped her hand so he could fetch the rope he had stored behind some discarded barrels and the loss of her touch swept through him. He didn't take her hand again. It was not necessary, and to take it would reveal too much of what was in his heart.

'This is the difficult part,' he said.

'Oh, good, because it's been very easy so far.'

He smiled as he looped the rope around his shoulders. 'If anything happens to me, take the rope and tie one to a merlon in the crenellations. Tug on it to make sure it can support your weight and then climb over the edge. Do not hesitate or wait. Just go.'

'Not without you,' she whispered.

'Yes, without me,' he countered firmly. 'Lord Cradoc

won't hesitate to punish you for this. You must promise me that you will go, whatever happens. If you don't, I will have risked my life for nothing.'

She was silent.

'Promise me, Ari. I don't want all of this to have been in vain.'

Her gaze was bleak as she looked at him but she said, 'I promise I will keep going.'

He nodded. 'Good. When we start to climb, we must make sure that we make no sound. I know where it is I wish us to make our descent, so follow me until I stop. Is there anything else you want to discuss before we begin?'

She shook her head. 'It's simple enough. Follow you in silence, climb down the wall using nothing but a bit of old rope. Escape.'

He smiled. 'Exactly.'

It wasn't until they were peering over the edge of the wall that Ari spoke again. 'Leo. I don't think I can do this.'

She was staring down to the darkness below. He glanced in the direction she was looking, his stomach twisted in familiar fear. The climb looked endless without the ground in sight.

'Yes, you can,' was all he said.

She shook her head. 'I thought I could, but I can't.' She was backing slowly away from where he was tying his knots.

He reached out and brushed the back of her hand, her fingers turned towards his and they slipped together as if they had been doing this their whole lives. She stepped up to him and rested her head in the crook of his neck.

'I know it's scary but at the bottom of this rope is everything you've always wanted. You're one climb away from freedom.'

She nodded against him.

'I know all that but I don't think my legs will carry me over the edge. My stepfather was right. I am too weak to be a warrior.'

'What did you tell me when I had a moment of doubt in the castle?'

'I can only think about falling to my death and can remember nothing of my life up until this point.'

He laughed and felt her shoulders shake as well. Good, she was not too far gone in her fear to have lost her sense of humour. He would be able to get her to take these last few steps. 'Telling yourself your stepfather was right about you is creating an enemy who is not here right now. Lord Owain ap Llewellyn did not know you, but I do. You are courageous and strong and loving and fierce. You can climb over the edge of the battlements, not because you are not scared but because you are a person who faces their fears head-on and makes a brave decision.

She let out a long breath and he knew she was all right. She was going to do it.

'Fine. But if I die, I will haunt you.'

'I'm counting on it. Come on. I'll help you.'

'What are you going to do?' She was gripping his arms.

'Keep watch.' He peeled her fingers off him. He didn't try to persuade her anymore, only acted as if she wasn't scared and this was commonplace. Even though he'd tied the rope tightly, he still held on to it as she began her descent. Watching her disappear into the darkness was one of the hardest things he had ever done. Waiting as the rope remained taut seemed to last for an eternity, and listening for a cry of fear or of triumph stretched what little was left of his rationality. He questioned every decision he had made as the moments wore on, and there was no sense of whether she had reached the bottom or whether she was dangling just out of sight, too petrified to move or call out.

When he thought he could no longer take it, the rope finally went slack. Without pausing for a moment, he followed her over the edge, heedless of the stones that scraped against him, thinking only of getting to her to check she was still in one piece. For the first time ever, he was not fearful of the height and he reached the bottom far quicker than he had imagined was possible.

As his feet touched the ground, arms were flung around him and he was held tightly.

'You made it.'

He laughed into her hair.

'Of course I did. I told you I would.'

He wanted to sink to the ground to cover her body with his and kiss her until neither of them could breathe. Instead, he said, 'We must keep going.'

She dropped her arms, not complaining that there was no time to rest or recover from the horrific climb. She would make an excellent soldier— No, he corrected himself, she *will* make an excellent soldier.

Moonlight illuminated their way and it was not far to the edge of the forest where he had tied up Bosco and Bel. It was a matter of moments to get them loose and then he and Ari were finally on their way.

Chapter Twenty

They rode through the night, not stopping even once to rest the horses. As dawn crept across the sky and there was still no sign of anyone pursuing them, Ari began to believe that they had done it.

As the sun rose higher, Leo brought the horses to a walk but they still did not stop and neither did they speak. He passed a water skin to her and she drank thirstily before handing it back, but that was the last of their interactions until the sun was high above them. It was then that Leo brought the horses to a complete stop.

He scratched his cheek, his gaze looking everywhere but at her.

'What is it?' she asked.

'We've reached a crossroads.'

She glanced about her at the two paths that led in different directions. 'I can see that,' she said, smiling at him.

He smiled back, the expression not quite reaching his eyes.

'That way,' he said, pointing towards the path that led to the east, 'lies England and Windsor. I have some clothes I can give you, to help with your disguise, although I would recommend binding your—' he gestured to her chest '—if you really want to get away with pretending to be a male. I don't know how you will hide the lack of beard or the fact that you are an incredibly beautiful woman for very long, but perhaps you already have a plan for that.'

Ari clutched her reins. That way lay freedom and all she had ever longed for. She should be exultant, but instead her heart hurt as if it were breaking into several pieces.

When she said nothing, he continued. 'This way lies my destination.' He gestured behind him. 'I must travel to meet my brother knights. I have given my word that I will help them with their missions and I cannot renege on that.'

She swallowed, those damned tears threatening again. It was as well they were going their separate ways. She'd not shed a tear for many years before she'd met him, but now tears were coming all the time. It was annoying.

She turned to look at the path she must take. It was long, and disappeared into the distance. It would be lonely but she was used to being by herself. She was fine—she was more than fine. She was…devastated. She did not want to leave Leo, did not know how she would give Bel the order to turn along the track away from him.

Behind her, Leo cleared his throat once, twice, a sure sign he was tense. If this was his way of saying goodbye, she didn't want him to start. Her neck was almost straining with the effort of not looking at him.

'You could come with me.' His words were spoken so softly that she almost missed them.

She turned to look at him, the expression on his face almost matching the feeling in her heart.

'What did you say?' she asked, needing to hear it again to be sure she had not dreamed it.

He cleared his throat and she hid a smile. 'I said that you could come with me, if you wanted.'

She nodded slowly, warmth unfurling within her. 'Is that what you would like?'

He ran a hand down his face and this time she did smile. He was quietly adorable when he was unsure of himself. His eyes narrowed when he caught sight of her face.

'Are you playing with me?' he asked, some of his normal teasing back in his voice.

That wiped the smile from her face. She didn't want him to feel as if she was not taking this seriously, not when this was potentially the most important decision of her life.

'No. At least, not exactly.' She inhaled deeply, pressing her hand to her chest in a futile gesture to stop her heart from hammering quite so quickly. 'If I come with you, I want to know whether it's because you want me with you or because it goes against your chivalric code of honour to leave a woman wandering the country alone.'

He grinned and her stomach turned over. She wondered how long it would take before the sight of his smile stopped making her body react like that. She hoped never. 'The country would be far more scared of you than you would be of it.'

'That's not an answer,' she said softly.

He shifted in his saddle. 'You're right, it's not. The thing is, Ari, I want you to have the future you deserve. I want you to be happy and fulfilled and I don't want to stop you because of my feelings for you.'

She rubbed her thumb along the length of Bel's reins. 'What feelings are those?'

For an endless moment, she thought he would not answer.

'I love you, Ari. I want you to stay with me. I want you to be my wife, to travel with me and to have a lifetime full of adventure, but because I love you, I also want you to be free, if that's what you want. I did not come to rescue you from Lord Cradoc just to possess you myself. The choice for your future is yours to make.'

She could hardly believe what she was hearing. 'You love me?'

He smiled. 'Yes.'

'And you want me to be your wife but you also want me to have adventures with you, not to stay at home and keep a household running for you.'

His smile deepened. 'I don't have a household for you to manage and I can't seem to keep you in one place, either. It would be better if you were with me. Besides, there is no one else I would want by my side in a sword fight. I—'

But Ari did not wait to hear any more. She launched herself off Bel's back towards him. He caught her awkwardly, laughing as he pulled her onto Bosco so that she was sitting facing backwards, her front plastered against his body.

She silenced his laughter by pressing an open-mouthed kiss to his jaw. She felt his rumble of satisfaction against her chest as she moved to claim his mouth. She was vaguely aware of Bosco beginning to move, the horse's steady gait swaying slowly beneath their bodies. She had no idea how long they kissed but eventually Leo lifted his head. His eyes were glazed and his lips swollen but he was still smiling.

'Is that a yes?'

'It's a yes.' She moved to take his mouth again, but he held her back.

'You do realise that we will have to be careful. That if you become my wife there can be no children between us while our lives are on a battlefield.'

She slipped her arms around his waist, nestling into the space between his chest and his neck, the space that seemed to be made just for her. 'Are you asking for my hand in marriage?'

'I thought that was a given.'

She looked up at him, her smile wide. 'I would love to be your wife.' His heart clenched tightly. 'As for children, are they something you have always longed for?'

'I have never expected to have them, as I never expected to have a wife either, but now I cannot imagine a life without you. If you'd chosen to go to Windsor you would probably have found me trailing pathetically after you in a heartsick manner.'

She laughed. She could not imagine Leo doing anything in a pathetic manner. 'I have always wanted to be a warrior and if we do not have children then I am fine with that. We can still enjoy each other, though, can't we?' She pressed herself against the length she could feel against her stomach.

'Mmm,' he said, pulling her even closer towards him. 'We shall have to be creative, that is all.'

'Shall we try out some of that creativeness right now?' she asked, lightly scraping her nails against the soft skin of his neck.

Leo pulled Bosco to a stop. 'I think that's the best idea you've had since I met you.'

He jumped down from his horse, carrying her with him, and for the rest of the day they proceeded to be very creative indeed.

Epilogue

'Did Mama really pose as a boy, Papa?'

Leo could understand his son's confusion. Seeing Ari rounded with their fourth child, her long hair in an elaborate braid, it was almost impossible to imagine a time when she had pretended to be a man so that they could fight alongside each other on the battlefield. That she had distinguished herself as one of the most elite fighters of the King's Army was a source of great pride to them both. It was a shame she'd had to hide her real identity, but together they had decided that it was safer that way.

Even now, she was teaching their oldest daughter the best way to hold a sword, despite the size of her stomach. Leo had to bite back a smile because she did not look comfortable or elegant, not the way she normally did when she wielded any weapon.

'Will you tell me the story of when you and Mama ran away from the bad man?' asked Lloyd.

Ari made her way over to them, with more of a waddle than a purposeful stride, and Leo dropped his head to hide a smirk. Oh, she would know what he was doing and she would pretend to get cross, and then there'd be teasing words between them and that always led to...

Well, there was a reason their fourth child was on the way when they'd sworn that three was ample.

'Your father and I never rode away from a bad man, Lloyd,' she said, ruffling their son's hair. 'We always ride *towards* danger.'

This time, Leo didn't hide his grin. They'd run away a fair few times. Good fighters had good battle sense and knew when all was lost. Ari had kept her flair for drama in the years they had been together.

'The time Mama was locked in a castle and you had to get her out.'

Ah, his children loved the story of how he and Ari had met. Maybe it was because he enjoyed embellishing his role in Ari's rescue, which led to private teasing between the two of them, which led to... He grinned and winked at her. Her eyes gleamed in response but before he could begin the tale, Ari started to speak and her version was just as embellished as his, only this time she had the leading role and he was a mere bit-player. The children had heard the story from both sides so many times that it wasn't long before they were calling for their favourite parts.

Leo sat back and watched his wife of nearly eighteen years. He loved the way she talked as much as he had in the beginning. She was coming to the crux of the tale now, her hands waving about in front of her face as she told of their flight. She'd stop there. They never told their children of the time they had spent together directly afterwards. That was for their own private recollections only, which always led to...

He scratched his chin. He was a very lucky man and

he knew it. Most things he and Ari did together led to their enjoying one another's bodies immensely.

They'd been married in a private ceremony, shortly after their escape, just the two of them so as not to draw attention to themselves. They had heard that Lord Cradoc sent hunting parties out into the surrounding forests for weeks afterwards, but of course there had been no trace of the runaway bride. They'd never heard anything about Lord Owain or Lady Katherine, and although that hurt Ari, Leo knew she liked to think her mother had had a good life with the many children she and Lord Owain had together. One of the tales that reached their ears was that Lady Arianwen had run off and died within a few days of her escape, killed by footpads or a wild beast. Leo's name had never been linked to the incident. Lord Cradoc had never taken a second wife, and his castle had gone to a neighbouring lord after his death.

'Papa.' His son tapped his chin, bringing Leo back to the moment. 'Can you teach me how to climb down the side of the castle wall?'

'Perhaps when you're older,' he said, smiling at his wife's anxious face. 'Now, it's time you went to sleep.'

'But it's still light outside.'

'Boys who want adventure know when to get a good rest,' Ari countered.

Lloyd and his siblings grumbled but eventually shuffled off to their own chamber, leaving Ari and Leo blissfully alone.

'Finally,' he murmured as the door closed.

'Why are you so desperate to get me by myself? Could it be you want to go over your technique?'

Ari picked up the play sword she'd been using with their daughter earlier and brandished it towards him.

'Not quite,' Leo said, plucking the wooden sword from her fingers and tugging Ari towards him. 'I was thinking it was time for a bit more creativity.' His hands slipped beneath her gown.

'Hmm,' she said, turning in his grip and brushing her lips against his. 'I know what we haven't tried in a while...'

* * * * *

*If you enjoyed this story,
keep an eye out for the next book in
Ella Matthews's
The Knights' Missions miniseries
coming soon!*

*While you wait,
check out her installment in the
Brothers and Rivals collection*
Her Warrior's Surprise Return

*Or immerse yourself in
The King's Knights miniseries*

The Knight's Maiden in Disguise
The Knight's Tempting Ally
Secrets of Her Forbidden Knight
Bound to the Warrior Knight